The Contract

T.G. Quinn   Elizabeth Lane

Cover illustration by Jack Carroll

Dedicated to the Dawg Pound

and to Red Right 88

April 17

Freshly cleaned uniforms smelled of Tide detergent as muddy cleats stomped through the house. The perfect scene of chaos was in full motion as Lisa tied up the end of Taylor's braid while yelling to Josh to grab a few Gatorades from the fridge in the garage. Their soccer game was at six o'clock, which meant the Chevy Suburban needed to be pulling out of the driveway by 5:30 p.m. to make it on time.

Lisa tried to check every to-do box in her head as she tied Taylor's shoe. Taylor was six years old and, in her mind, had just mastered the art of bunny style to tie her shoes. However, mastered is not the same word that came to her mother's mind. Time was of the essence so Taylor's bunny style technique would have to wait.

"Okay Gatorades, snacks, cleats, shin guards. Check, check, check," Lisa listed while struggling to put her jacket on.

"Come on Josh! We are going to be late for your game," she exclaimed. The scurrying of cleats against the hardwood was the sound of the message being received.

"Sorry mom. I was just grabbing your umbrella just in case the weatherman is right today," Josh said out of breath from his race down the stairs.

Josh was nine years old, placing him in the responsible, older brother role as soon as Taylor was born. Despite the typical nine-year-old tantrums due to tiredness, lack of attention, or a younger sister poking at him too much that day, Josh was a well-behaved, responsible kid. Sometimes he would be quiet, letting Taylor take center stage during dinner conversations, but his eyes were never oblivious. The weather. Of course, Josh checked the weather this morning.

"Oh my goodness, Josh, you are my lifesaver! I would have walked out without that," Lisa said with a sigh of relief.

As she was walking towards the garage door, her eyes caught a glimpse of a notification popping up on the top right-hand side of her computer sitting on the kitchen counter:

From: Marla Everson

Subject: PTO Meeting

That one will have to wait. She closed the lid of her laptop hoping that would pause the mass of emails that she has to read every day. Seatbelts were buckled and the blaring of the radio caused Lisa to jump. She turned the knob from volume 32 to volume 21.

"Oh, come on Mom! Party pooper! I need some warmup music mom!" Josh protested.

"And I need my ear drums to last me another forty years thank you very much," Lisa replied.

A compromise was made at Volume 25. Their Hunter Green Chevy Suburban pulled away from the dark red brick house they called home at 28924 Inglewood Dr. in Bay Village, Ohio, a suburb located thirteen miles west of downtown Cleveland. Josh was busy syncing his lips to the lyrics from the radio while Taylor entertained her mother with an abundance of questions during the car ride.

"Hey mommy. Will daddy get to see me play goalie today?" Taylor questioned with big, hopeful eyes. As the Suburban approached a red light, Lisa reached for her phone and clicked to her messages with her husband, Darian.

"Taylor plays on field three at 6 p.m. Josh plays on field two at 7 p.m. I have a chair for you."

The message read delivered below the blue iMessage bubble.

"Of course, sweetie. He is going to meet us there after work," Lisa responded.

The party of three pulled in through the opened white gates of Cahoon Park in suburban Bay Village. With a horizon of soccer fields coming into view, Lisa glanced at her iPhone…

5:42 pm…. Just made it.

"Keep your eyes peeled for field three, Taylor," Lisa said.

"To the right mom. There is a spot next to that blue van," Josh pointed out. Lisa smiled at her son's directions. He was on it again. Taylor hopped out with a red Gatorade in one hand and a soccer ball tucked under her right armpit. Josh started loading up his small, but mighty shoulder with the two foldable chairs for his parents.

"Good luck Taylor!" Lisa shouted. "Thanks Josh. Let's go find a place for our seats."

The referee blew his whistle causing the blue team to begin the game with an opening kick. Darian was late and Lisa was not surprised.

After being married for 12 years, Lisa had a good grasp on her husband's behavior and habits, both the good and the bad. She even joked to him that one day he'll even be late for his own funeral.

****

The late autumn winds whipped fiercely across State Street toward Washtenaw Ave, teasing the students with a taste of what the upcoming winter at the University of Michigan was going to be like.   Professor Mayfield's Entrepreneur business lecture was in Mason Hall, only a stone's throw away from most of the dorms. The cool winds somehow made the walk seem a little longer.

Not exactly the ideal setting for the traditional love story of boy spots girl, boy talks to girl, boy asks girl to study, boy and girl catch feelings for each other, boy and girl live happily ever after. That plotline expired in the eighties. The reality was Darian Reilly found himself buried in his MacBook reviewing previous lecture notes to even realize the stunning sorority president of Alpha Chi Omega. She was doing that thing with her eyes that examines a person from head to toe and back again. Her cherry blossom perfume and the not-so-subtle eyeballing of Darian did not stand a chance against how to code the restoration of files that the PowerPoint slide was presenting.

For Darian, girls had infrequently crossed or lingered on his mind. As a twenty-year-old in college, the closest thing to a date that Darian experienced was a playdate with Pam from a few doors down in the third grade. Sharing goldfish and letting her take a turn on his new red razor blade scooter was the peak of Darian's flirtation skills with women. In his mind, women were just a distraction, and the president of Alpha Chi Omega sitting two seats away was proving his stubborn point.

Most young boys grow up wanting to be a firefighter, a police officer, or an athlete. At kindergarten graduation Darian answered the "what do you want to be when you grow up" question with 'an entrepreneur'. His young mind did not stand a chance at spelling out that word, however, he understood that an entrepreneur was someone who started their own business and that idea settled nicely with him. At the time, the only business he had hopes of starting up was a lemonade stand at the same corner where he would wait for the bus in the mornings.

In middle school stereotype terms, Darian was the bookworm. However, his mother's cheekbones and father's bright blue eyes made him a bookworm with a pretty face. He caught the eye of many ladies, but his eyes were always distracted with words in a book, the pieces of a new project, or the slides on a PowerPoint lecture. So, Darian just continued taking notes on the process of buying and expanding businesses as the chestnut brown curls bounced a few seats down.

A dishwater blonde ponytail rested high on a girl's head in the front row of the lecture. Her hair looked like it was on the verge of needing a shower or dry shampoo while her sweatpants and oversized sweatshirt screamed "*I set my alarm for ten minutes before class because I am not a morning person.*" Her hair would have blended in with all the other ponytails in the lecture if it were not for the ambitious and frequent hand that raised next to it.

Despite her lazy fashion attire when it came to her academics, Lisa Baker was anything but lazy. She was the student who dug deeper than the rest to fully grasp a concept or challenged an idea by asking "why" when most college students would be responding to the latest notification buzzing on their phone. Lisa's dream job when she was a tiny kindergartener was to be a teacher. Organization came naturally to her at a young age, and she had a heart that wished to help people. Just like in Professor Mayfield's lecture, her curiosity always caused her to stand out and led her to a leadership position for the school newspaper and scholars club in high school. Her role in her high school friend group was the investigator because she always had to dive below the surface which made her an ambitious student inside the classroom and a certified snooper outside of it. Whenever one of her friends met a new boy, they would text Lisa his name and she would use the magical, yet terrifying Instagram app and the internet to learn more about the potential love interest of her friend. Although this investigative superpower of hers assisted her friends and their love lives, it tended to hurt her own. Lisa would go on dates with boys throughout high school and into college and know almost every small talk answer about the boy sitting across the restaurant table or beside her in the theater recliner.

Yeah, I played football back in high school. Let me guess, you wore jersey number 22.

Of course, these details remained inside the depths of Lisa's mind and never on her tongue. Instead, a question with an answer was posed to continue the conversation.

"What high school did you go to?" she posed. He went to Dearborn Heights, according to his Instagram bio.

"Dearborn Heights," he replied.

Lisa was convinced after a few dates with different guys that she should be hired by the FBI. The beneficial side of her curiosity was that it interested her in school and engaged her with the material which led her to her front row seat in a two-hundred-person lecture.

By now the PowerPoint had advanced to the discussion of bankruptcy in small businesses and large corporations and their different effects they each have on the companies and the consumer. There goes Lisa's hand.

"I'm just curious, what are the big hints that foreshadow the failure of a company?" Lisa questioned. "Oh, and also when a company is experiencing a downfall what is the best strategy to align it back on stable tracks?"

Ten rows back, Darian's fingertips were typing away. He addressed the heading of his new page, "Failure and Recovery of a Company." Bullet points were inserted on the blank page and "Sign #1" followed the first black dot.

"That's a good question, Lisa," Professor Mayfield commented. "The biggest sign of struggle for a company and its success would be competition. If there is high competition or bigger corporations that have a larger brand name, then it challenges the smaller company to stand out. Oftentimes the smaller, lesser-known company cannot afford the same technology and tactics that a larger, well-known company can which begin the downfall of the smaller company."

Darian's fingers went to work typing in the answer to Lisa's question and filling in the rest of the outline that the professor had

11

routinely provided the day before his lectures took place. After 90 minutes the lecture concluded, and most of the students had already made it to the line at the coffee shop right outside the lecture hall.

No, Darian did not turn around too fast, spill coffee on Lisa's sweatshirt, and fall in love. That love story was impossible these days because college students protected their cup of coffee just as much as their phones. Darian found Lisa in front of him waiting in another line: the line to ask Professor Mayfield a question post-lecture that often resulted in the same answer, "Come see me during office hours." No, Darian and Lisa did not bond over having the same question for their instructor, study together, and fall in love.

Instead, their fathers found themselves in the same Friday golf league at Evergreen Hills Country Club in Southfield, Michigan and became good friends. A devious plan on the twelfth hole putting green was made to set up the two love deprived twenty-year-olds.

One wedding, a mortgage and two kids later, Darian and Lisa Reilly were living the American dream. He graduated with a Software Engineering degree and started DigiNet, a company which monitors computer and internet security breaches for business and government. Lisa, no slouch herself with the computer, became a systems programmer and dabbled in email design and security.

They were inseparable. Life in Bay Village afforded them a wonderful lifestyle. While Darian was running DigiNet, Lisa kept busy running the house, taking care of Josh and Taylor, as well as doing some free-lance email consulting on the side. At times it seemed they didn't even have time to spit. But Lisa always said that's what keeps them young. They frequently went to dinner with friends and even socialized with some of the DigiNet people, including Gerry, his right-hand man at DigiNet and his wife, Nancy.

The next morning, the incessant ringing of his iPhone alarm went off promptly at 6:00 am. Darian, still a bit foggy, got up, showered and dressed to get to the office extra early. For today was the meeting he had scheduled with TRW, a firm whose client base had been compromised and was looking for a software firm who could provide an ample amount of IT and Internet protection. Darian knew if he got in front of the right people at TRW, the contract would be his.

This afternoon, he was going to be in front of the right people....

As he was leaving, he grabbed his old backpack which should have been detonated years ago, blew Lisa a kiss, slammed down the rest of his OJ and nearly tripped over Neely, their two-year-old Irish Setter as he headed to the office. Lisa, fighting off the temptation to climb back into bed for a few more winks before the kids got up, dove into the laundry, featuring Josh's grass-stained soccer uniform from the night before. Although it was only 6:33 am, it was never too early to check email, as far as she was concerned.

Email was her life. She was fascinated by it. All through college she was fixated on it thinking it to be the communication wave of the future and beyond. She was excited she could make a career out of being an email consultant. Many times, she would help Darian track down the source of a potential client by using some of the email tricks of the trade she had mastered. If Darian ever had a girlfriend on the side, she laughed to herself, he better not even think of emailing her!

Both Taylor and Josh showed up in the kitchen a few minutes after 7:00 am to eat their breakfast. Lisa juggled some last-minute test questions with Josh, along with getting the kitchen cleaned up prior to taking the kids to school. Although Normandy Elementary School was less than three miles away, instead of the bus, she enjoyed driving them there as it gave them a few extra minutes together. Out the door as the clock struck 7:30 am, Taylor and Josh jumped into their mom's car. Since it was still a cool April morning and looked like rain, the kids grabbed their jackets which were strewn about in the back seat. As they approached Normandy, there were more car riders than walkers, so the drop offline was longer than usual. Both gave mom a kiss and bolted into the main entrance of the school before the rain hit. Lisa turned and headed for home.

DigiNet was not a large company. With only a handful of employees, everyone had each other's back and seemed to work well together. Karen was the receptionist who always greeted everyone with a smile, whether it be by phone, skype or in person. Lori handled the office duties which basically meant if someone had a question, go to Lori. Gerry had met Darian shortly after he had moved to Ohio. He worked as a software engineer and designer out of school then came onboard with Darian when he formed DigiNet several years ago. Gerry and Darian were good friends and Gerry's wife Nancy got to be good friends with Lisa. The company was young but growing. Darian paid his employees very well, in addition to providing Lisa and the kids with a very comfortable lifestyle.

But something was missing. Darian needed that one big break in order to get DigiNet into the big time. He had read on the web that a large internationally known company had experienced some security breaches. They were a large local corporation, but he thought if given the chance to show what DigiNet could do to protect them, they would definitely like what they see.

And now, that company, TRW was seated in DigiNet's waiting room....

"Come in, gentlemen," Darian said as he motioned the two distinguished looking men into his conference room. DigiNet did not have large offices, however, they were very elegantly decorated and styled, largely due to the efforts of Gerry's wife, Nancy. "You must be Bob Clifford," said Darian.

"Yes, he replied. "This is Bill Hegarty, our Vice President of IT,"

Bob was the CFO of TRW who had recently been promoted following a recent corporate shakeup at the company. Gerry joined the meeting with the other men seated around the circular conference table. Although Darian was no slouch when it came to IT, he knew Gerry had a far better handle on what problems and issues had been occurring at TRW, so he mostly sat and listened while Gerry and Bill got into a deeper discussion on internet security and breaches. After several long and lengthy hours of discussions on malware, hard drive contamination, log file backup failures and cyber security biometrics, it seemed as though Bob and Bill were asking more of the right questions. Gerry was direct and matter of fact with them, something Darian sensed they had appreciated.

"Forgive me if I sound condescending, Bob said, "but for a small company, you really know your stuff when it comes to the issues we've been experiencing and what we apparently have been lacking."

"Quite frankly, Darian interjected, "although we are not as large as some of our competition, this allows our customers to come right to the decision maker and quickly make any changes or modifications they need. In your case, we could tell right away that your log files were contaminated and needed to be scrubbed before your employees performed any additional downloads, making the situation worse."

"Thank you, Darian," came Bob's reply. With a firm handshake the two TRW decision makers assured him that they will be hearing from them very shortly. After watching their car pull out of the parking lot, Darian and Gerry could hardly contain their sense of cautious optimism.

"Remember, warned Darian. "This is Cleveland."

"I know, I know" Gerry snapped back half smiling.

"The Drive"

"The Shot"

"The Fumble"

Gerry's halfhearted reference to nothing-ever-good-happens-to-Clevelanders by mentioning three of the most famous sports heartbreaking moments in the city's history did not go unnoticed by his colleague. Nonetheless, the two men had a little pep in their step the rest of the day. Darian stayed late to catch up on some other projects and darkness had set in over Northern Ohio as he headed for home.

April 19

"So, how did it go?" asked Lisa the next morning. Since Darian had arrived home shortly before eleven the night before, Lisa had already gone to bed.

"I thought it went as well as it could possibly go" he replied.

One thing about Darian and Lisa, good or bad, right or wrong, they always were up front with each other. No surprises, just the facts. Made life a lot simpler. Lisa knew that as soon as Darian would hear something, he would let her know.

"I really hate getting overly excited about something which may never materialize," he said. "But if this does happen…. his voice trailed off as he watched his pretty wife place her finger over her lips as if to say shhhhhh.

Darian knew his wife better than anyone and realized that in one simple gesture, she was reminding him to relax and take it one step at a time. He gave her a big kiss then hustled off to work reminding her he would be home for dinner.

The meeting with TRW actually went better than Darian let on with Lisa, or so he thought. He and Gerry were able to show them where their security breaches were and how to circumvent them, as well as others in the future. The fact that the two men from TRW told Darian they really liked what they saw in DigiNet and would get back to them within the next several weeks made Darian overly optimistic. This was good news, he thought even though he knew it would be a while before they received any word on a decision.

Arriving at his office shortly before 7:30 Darian glanced at his calendar and noticed it was relatively unfilled; it gave him a chance to catch up on efforts to pursue other client deals which were still in the works but had been put off.

The Lorain County Sheriff's Department had sent in a request for a bid on IT security. They were in the process of updating their entire computer aided dispatch system and needed some expertise along the way. Not a huge deal for DigiNet but it would help continue to pay the bills. The Sheriff was able to secure additional funding through the county levy which had just been passed the previous November and were ready to move forward with securing bids for the project. The deadline for the bid submission was July 1 so Darian knew he had a little time to move on this.

The City of Lakewood was going through a massive revamping of their police, fire and city administration computer networking system. Since the city had sold the old Lakewood Hospital to the Cleveland Clinic, it now had the funding available to move forward on these improvements.

The local Lakewood Court system, old and outdated and in serious need of improvement, was included as well.

Lakewood High School, the home of the Rangers, had also been included as part of the revitalization project. The City had made vast improvements on various historical monuments from Birdtown to the Gold Coast all the way to the corner of Elmwood and Madison. Now they were focusing their attention on the City's networking system and the improvements were necessary.

The City of North Olmsted was trying to find a way to link their historic bus line to City of Cleveland's bus lines, as well as the Regional Transit Authority's train system. North Olmsted was one of the first cities in the United States to operate its own bus line. Founded in 1931, the entire system had made several attempts over the years to be computerized but had always failed, nonetheless.

Located seventeen miles southwest of downtown Cleveland, North Olmsted was a mecca for young families to live and grow. It had North Olmsted Park which was always busy in the summer with kids sports and handicrafts and the North Olmsted Recreation Center which had indoor and outdoor pools in the summertime and two huge ice-skating rinks and toboggan sled runs for winter enjoyment. Great Northern Mall, one of the very first malls to be opened in the country over fifty years ago, was also in need of revitalization. The North Olmsted bus line for years made it very convenient for commuters to live in this fashionable suburb and yet work in downtown Cleveland conveniently. Since its acquisition by RTA, the funding was now in place for the bus line's improvements.

Numerous other projects were flashing across Darian's screen as he attempted to focus on which ones made the best sense for DigiNet and which ones were to be discarded. As he was updating his emails to check on the morning news items, a look of concern came over his face. He received an alert that Media Trex, one of DigiNet's competitors, had just received the inside track to do all the IT security work for Cleveland Health Alliance for the next four years. Cleveland Health Alliance was a group of 17 hospitals and over 300 physicians.

Darian's heart sank. He had been working on Cleveland Health Alliance for eight months and thought he had this one. It represented a sizable gain for his company if he were to win that contract. Now it was lost.

He reviewed his notes and files going back and forth trying to determine what went wrong with the Cleveland Health Alliance deal. His objective was to always try to learn from his experiences so he could prevent a similar deal from happening in the future.

"Media Trex is spread so thin already, " said Gerry as he wandered into Darian's office. "Their customers' biggest complaints are the lack of attention and support they provide. "Once CHA gets a taste of Media Trex' lack of customer support, they'll wish they had come on over to our side," he said.

"I hear you," echoed Darian. "But that doesn't help us much now. Just wish I knew what caused them to choose those guys over us."

"They were snowed by Media Trex' dog and pony show boss." They're like that copier company you hear advertising ten times a day on the radio about how great their service is and yet most of their customers can't stand them" Gerry replied.

Darian knew this was a setback but certainly not an insurmountable one. He still had enough irons in the fire and a few possible deals waiting in the wings to provide him with a resurgence of energy. However, this made the TRW deal even that much more significant. If DigiNet is awarded the TRW contract, then life is good, and the company is on its way. If not, well then, it's time to head for the 480 bridge!

JK.... LMAO he laughed to himself....

Darian had jumped into his car and was heading back to the office when it sounded like his phone would not stop. He played racquetball at River Oaks in Rocky River on Wednesdays at noon with his neighbor, Jack Flynn and always left his phone in the car. Gerry had been trying to reach him. Great. Finally, we get the green light on the TRW deal, Darian thought. CALL ME ASAP was the text from Gerry. Darian headed for the office and dialed Gerry on his cell.

"What is it," he asked Gerry. Did the TRW deal finally come through?

Gerry had explained that no they had not heard back from TRW yet but the contract DigiNet had with Cuyahoga county was due to expire in two weeks and they had not heard back from anyone as of yet.

"Not to worry, came Darian's patient reply. The county is always short of manpower due to budget constraints and so they always wait until the last few days to announce their renewals. I'll call Sheppard and see where things are. The whole deal just needs his signature and we're good to go for the next four years."

James Sheppard had been the Cuyahoga County commissioner for twenty-seven years. Darian got to know him when he did an internship under Sheppard after he first graduated from Michigan. Almost like a father figure to Darian, Sheppard also had hired him to perform landscaping duties at his lakefront home out in Bay Village. Darian spent several summers working on the multi-level terraces and the jetty beach below at the Sheppard home and eventually developed a mutual respect with his elder friend. Once Darian was commissioned to tear up the Sheppard's ancient asphalt driveway with nothing more than a pickax and two 30-gallon buckets. He couldn't decide which was worse, carrying two buckets of broken asphalt weighing 70 pounds each *down* the sixty-two stairs to the beach or climbing back *up* those same sixty-two stairs fighting exhaustion!

Sheppard knew DigiNet had done a great job while they had the Cuyahoga county contract. He trusted Darian and always knew he could count on him even if it meant going beyond the call of duty. They even ran into each other in Bay Village from time to time when Darian and Lisa were out walking Josh as a baby. Sheppard and his wife Rebecca even had the Reillys over for an occasional cook out at their lakefront home.

Darian left a voice message for Sheppard as he drove back to the office. He had other pressing deals to go over and Cuyahoga County still belonged to DigiNet. Upon arriving at the office, he noticed Gerry at his desk with a somber look on his face.

"What is it", Darian asked. "You are not going to believe this," Gerry replied. He flipped his laptop sideways giving Darian full view of the message.

The County had issued an email saying they are not going to renew. Cuyahoga County was the largest customer of DigiNet and had been since Darian started the company. When he looked over the entire message, he read where James Sheppard was retiring and the new county commissioner, Ed Blackwell had already made arrangements with another firm to provide their web and IT security.

Darian was stunned. He had to think clearly and move fast. He called Sheppard again from his cell and was finally able to reach him.

"It was clear politics, pure and simple," Sheppard said to Darian, returning his call.

As it turns out Blackwell was introduced to the CEO of Media Trex, Sam Jenkins at the wedding of Blackwell's daughter. Jenkins just "happened" to be at the wedding and convinced Blackwell that DigiNet was the devil. Furthermore, Jenkins also had a friend who owned a travel agency in Rocky River and was able to provide a nice honeymoon package to Blackwell's daughter, at no charge of course. This was all off the record, but Darian believed every word Sheppard was saying. After he hung up, he tried to reach Blackwell but to no avail. The news was confirmed later that afternoon when Darian and Gerry saw it on the local 6 o'clock news. Now the TRW people had to come through....

May 14

It had been a long week for DigiNet, but Darian did not let on to Lisa about the obvious disappointments he had experienced at the office. However, she did notice that he just did not appear to be his usual fun-loving self at certain times. They both loved the water and would frequently take Josh and Taylor to nearby Huntington Beach for an evening of ice cream and relaxation. He didn't want to let on to her that the Cleveland Health Alliance and Cuyahoga County both slipped through his fingers. He just kept telling her the TRW deal was taking longer than expected. When she asked if everything else was ok with the company he replied with a simple "everything is fine." One of the delights Darian enjoyed this time of year was being able to hclp coach Josh's little league team. It allowed him to keep his mind off things at the office for a while.

Darian had grown up playing baseball since he was eight years old. He loved to hit right from the start and was rather good at it. Even though the rules said you had to be nine to play on a little league team, he was able to join as an eight-year-old. As much as he loved the game, occasionally it did not love him back. Once, back in high school in a game at Bedford Woods Park in Southfield, Michigan, he took a fastball right in the left forearm. Fractured ulna. Out six weeks. Another time while attempting to score from second to home, while sliding into the plate he caught the catcher's shin guard and heard a "pop." Fractured ankle. Out for the season.

But Darian's competitive spirit from baseball and sports spilled over into his studies and later his career. Figuring his achievements in his studies would bring him greater rewards than in sports, he became an A student much throughout high school and later college. Once Lisa saw Josh take his first turn at bat in T-Ball, she realized the apple didn't fall too far from the tree!

If Josh was the athlete in the family, then Taylor was the intellectual. She was rarely seen without something to read, even if it was her brother's empty bottle of Gatorade! Although she just turned six, Taylor was able to read and comprehend at a nine-year-old level. Not nearly athletically gifted as her older brother, she still was able to carry on a conversation with several of Darian and Lisa's friends, much to their amazement. She could remember dates and facts which made her popular even among several of Josh's friends. As the school year was drawing to a close, Taylor was already bugging her mom about scheduling her for the upcoming summer reading program at Huntington Park. Lisa and Darian realized they probably won't have to worry about college expenses when it comes time for Taylor to decide where to go.

But Darian had other things to worry about. He and Lisa had always enjoyed a gracious lifestyle and rarely wanted for much. Although they were not wealthy, they seldom thought twice about spending on themselves or the kids. They did have some money saved, however, like many young couples it seemed their household expenses would always continue to chip away at what little of a nest egg they had accumulated.

The Reillys were planners and extremely diligent about maintaining a successful strategy for mapping out their future. They both knew that life would eventually throw them a few curves whether it be unexpected medical expenses, lack of available scholarship funds or a downturn in the economy.

Several years earlier Lisa was the victim of an identity stalker. Someone had gained access to her credit file, including bank cards and account numbers. After months of phone calls, emails and discussions with Society Bank, they were able to rectify her financial status and correct all the misinformation which had taken place. However, Lisa's credit history had been tarnished and that was something she and Darian had to work through. They both knew that maintaining their positive credit status was imperial to getting where they wanted to be.

Darian did the same for his company. At DigiNet, the company enjoyed an exceptionally good credit rating by paying their bills on time and not borrowing unless it was absolutely necessary. He had constantly been receiving solicitations from numerous competitive banks asking for DigiNet's business, but he was always loyal in his personal and professional relationships. The dual loss of Cleveland Health Alliance and Cuyahoga County clearly represented a sizable blow to DigiNet. However, Darian always took the long-term perspective and realized that these two items represented one of the many valleys he would have to endure as well as the peaks he would be able to enjoy. However, things were beginning to slow down. It became obvious to him that DigiNet might have to start cutting back, and the Reillys may have to as well....

The fourth Friday in the month of May marked the unofficial beginning of summer as it was the Friday of the Memorial Day weekend. Over the years Cleveland had always been known for its long, harsh winters but come the end of May, the summer was kicked off with a vengeance. The weatherman promised a beautiful three-day holiday weekend and the Reillys were planning to take advantage of every minute. They had plans for a neighborhood grille out on Friday with Darian as the master chef, a day trip to Put-in-Bay Island on Saturday and an all-day boat ride with Jack and Anna Flynn on Jack's 32-foot Sea Ray powerboat *Social Distance* on Sunday. The whole neighborhood was filled with sounds of lawn mowers, hustle bustle at the grocery and hardware stores and even the familiar sound of the first place Cleveland Indians being broadcast on the radio.

"I'm on my way home now" Darian replied to his impatient wife.

Lisa had invited several of the neighbors over for a Friday night Memorial Day weekend cookout and her grille master husband was still at the office.

"Maggie and Joel are on their way over so can you please pick up some extra beer on your way home?" Lisa asked.

"No problem honey" replied Darian as he jumped into his Audi. "Anything else?"

"No" replied Lisa "but hit the gas because everyone will be here shortly. But don't kill yourself coming home on Lake Road."

Quickly realizing that the weekend had already begun, Darian stopped at the neighborhood Heinens grocery store, grabbed a few cases of Stella and White Claw and headed for home. Maggie loved her White Claw and Joel never met a bottle of Stella he didn't like.

Arriving shortly before 6pm, he was greeted by his wife and two kids bounding out the back door. Almost on cue, the Baileys arrived with a hand pulled cooler filled with adult beverages along with their white lab, Lady.

"Ahoy matey" came Joel's greeting as they made it to the backyard.

"Ahoy yourself" Darian shot back playfully. "Come aboard, mate and help yourself to a cold one."

Maggie and Joel Bailey had been married for three years. Both were finishing up their graduate studies, hers in chemistry and his in biology. They had met at Cleveland State as lab partners and were inseparable ever since. Though they were yet to have any children,

Maggie made sure she had packed plenty of child beverages to take the pressure off Lisa.

"I guess it'll take a couple of Irishmen to get the party started, eh?" Joel asked.

"Sure, and it will be a fine piece of magic" Darian replied with his best Irish brogue. "And the Mrs. is looking radiant, Mr. Bailey," he added.

"Sure, and begorrah" Joel replied in his own fake Irish brogue. "Your lass is looking more beautiful than a fine Dublin sunset," he quipped. The two neighborhood buddies laughed at their foolishness and then toasted to the beautiful Cleveland weekend which lay ahead.

Shortly thereafter, the O'Malleys and the Peterjohns had arrived, and the party was on. Conversations ranged from the upcoming summer camps and activities for the children to the first place Cleveland Indians and the Cavs getting closer to the NBA finals. A mild breeze off the lake kept the evening nice and temperate as the adults congregated in the Reilly's screened in patio while the children played several versions of "Ghost in the Graveyard" utilizing several of the neighborhood backyards. Joel, always the prankster, warned all the kids not to wander too far as the ghost of Dr. Sam may come back to haunt them.

"Stop" yelled Maggie as she pleaded with her husband to refrain from scaring all the neighborhood kids with a story from the famous 1954

Bay Village murder. "We would like to keep these people as our friends, Joel" she quipped.

More laughter, stories and memories filled the evening until one by one each couple eventually headed for home. Maggie insisted on staying behind to help the Reilly's clean up the kitchen, but Lisa thanked her for the kids' drinks and said she probably should make sure Joel makes the three door walk home safely. Darian and Lisa made a valiant effort to clean and pick up then collapsed into bed shortly before midnight.

As the sun broke through the windows and the sound of the waves came from the lake below, the Reillys were off for their annual Saturday Memorial Day Weekend day trip at Put-in-Bay island, about an hour drive west of Bay Village. Darian and Lisa had frequented the island numerous times during their years together and, according to legend, he took her to the Round House on their very first date. It was already a little after 8am and Josh and Taylor were ready to go. Lisa had made sure all the doors and windows were locked lest a sudden storm may arrive which frequently happens when living near the shores of Lake Erie.

As she grabbed a few road breakfast snacks for the kids to have for the trip, Darian was leaving some last-minute dog instructions for Paul, the O'Malley's thirteen-year-old neighborhood son who would be looking after Neely. Paul was familiar with the drill, as he had been commissioned by the Reillys numerous times in the past to watch and care for their Irish setter. He also knew the Reillys usually got home from Put-In-Bay much later than expected, largely due to the overabundance of ice cream and fudge shops on the way home throughout Marblehead, Port Clinton and Sandusky.

"We should have taken my car," Darian remarked as they pointed the Chevy Suburban westbound on I-90.

"No way, Lisa shot back, firmly. "While yours might be fun to drive to the office and back, mine is the *ultimate* road car."

"As usual, you are right honey" Darian responded sheepishly.

"Thank you, darlin" Lisa, murmured back to her husband with that patented smile and a twinkle in her eye.

Traffic on I-90 that Saturday morning was light and the promise of good weather for the day gave the Reilly family a sense of excitement as they headed west. Ever since they had moved to Greater Cleveland, they were sure of one thing when it comes to weather: You can *never* be sure. But the forecast was great, the sun was out, and they were on their way. Passing through Vermillion, then Huron and on through Sandusky, Darian and Lisa engaged in some quiet conversation about the party last night.

Josh was busy with his headphones trying to make sense out of his latest Mario game he had recently downloaded. Darian and Lisa were very strict with their kids when it came to grades and education. The deal with Josh was that he was allowed to get one B on his final report card for the year and the rest had to be all As. If he were able to do so he would be rewarded with a new video game which he could download. Not wanting to miss an opportunity, Josh came home on the last day of school with all

As and quickly reminded his mom of the deal they had made. Lisa gave him the green light to download the game and remarked suspiciously how quickly it was for Josh to download such a large file. Hmmmm, she thought to herself.

Taylor was busy immersed in her summer reading book, *Alice in Wonderland* and nearly oblivious to her surroundings. Although she loved traveling with her family on day trips either to Put-In-Bay or in the other direction to Conneaut, Ohio where Lisa's parents lived, she kept herself buried inside some sort of reading material. Just finishing up the first grade, Taylor was always anxious to get started on her next level of academics. To her the summer was an ok time but she couldn't wait to get back to the classroom in the fall.

The bright sunlight suddenly shone through the car windows. The Reillys were turning north bound on to the Edison Bridge over the Sandusky Bay. With the morning sun reflecting off the beautiful bay water, it was nearly blinding to glance eastward into the light. A few water skiers and several boaters were spotted below. It looked as though one of the skiers was headed toward the ski jump, but the Suburban was traveling faster than the small boat below and quickly landed on the other end of the Edison Bridge, and into Port Clinton. Once a small fisherman town, Port Clinton, Ohio had grown as a mini vacation spot for travelers from Ohio,

Michigan and other neighboring states. Catching a Lake Erie bass, walleye or bluegill had become a very popular attraction over the years and hotels, bed-n-breakfasts and condos were popping up everywhere.

Meandering their way through the historic streets of Port Clinton, Darian finally steered the car on to Catawba Island where they were to catch the Miller ferry boat across Lake Erie onto Put-In-Bay. Heading north on Ohio Route 53 they heard that familiar sound of the horn that signaled the arrival of the William Miller Ferry boat. "Look, there's a parking spot straight ahead under that pine tree" Lisa exclaimed. Not wanting to waste any time and miss this ferry, Darian dispensed with backing the Suburban into the parking spot and simply pulled right in.

"Let's go, guys" said Lisa as the family raced down the end of the road as the ferry was starting to load cars on.

"Can we go watch the cars load onto the boat?" pleaded Josh.

"I'll get the tickets," Darian commanded as he nodded to Lisa. You guys go with mom and I'll be right there".

The very idea of cars driving onto a boat was fascinating to young Josh and he didn't want to miss a moment of it. The familiar smell of Lake Erie fish was now upon them as they watched car after car being loaded onto the ferry boat. As the last car was loaded on, the motorcycles and finally the cyclists followed up just as the pedestrians started to walk on.

"Here we are, Daddy" shout Taylor as she waved to get Darian's attention.

Without saying a word, Lisa waved her husband over to the walk-on entrance. One by one they each handed the gatekeeper their one-way ticket and were on the boat.

Almost instinctively, the family of four headed up the nearby staircase and were standing at the very top, near the captain looking down on the scenery below. The wind had always seemed to pick up as is customary when traveling near the Lake Erie Islands and today was no exception. But the sun was shining, the air was warm, and the promise of a fun day lay ahead. Suddenly there was a familiar swaying amongst the passengers which meant the boat was free, the engine roared and was now headed to Put-In-Bay. Although only an 18-minute trip across the water to the Island, for a couple of six- and nine-year-old kids, it seemed like an eternity! Darian and Lisa were veterans of this scene. Many times, they had made the trip either by themselves or with friends and sometimes even stayed overnight in neighboring Port Clinton. At times they would rent bikes or a golf cart or simply take the shuttle into town. With the kids they always rented bikes with seats on the back but now that Josh and Taylor were older, they rented a golf cart which allowed them to cover more ground on the island and made touring that much more fun.

The Great Lakes can be a harsh reminder of how cold and cruel old man winter can be. Back on November 9, 1975 the bulk cargo freighter *Edmund Fitzgerald*, once the largest ship on the entire Great Lakes, embarked on a trip from Superior, Wisconsin to Detroit, Michigan. But the ship never reached its destination. On November 10th, a storm with hurricane force winds and thirty-five-foot waves sent the ship to its watery grave 530 feet to the bottom of Lake Superior. All twenty-nine on board had perished.

Lake Erie sported a number of different islands, both on the Canadian and the American side. The three main islands on the American side are North Bass Island, also known as the Isle of St. George, Middle Bass Island and South Bass Island also known as Put-In-Bay Island. Neighboring Kelley's Island was also an immensely popular vacation and fishing spot.

But Put-In-Bay is *the* quintessential hot spot for family, friends, food and fun. From the onset of Memorial Day weekend to the end of Labor Day in September, it is always a party at Put-In-Bay. Once a sleepy little island occupied by early Native Americans and then a gateway for fur traders, the war of 1812 changed all that. Led by Commodore Oliver Hazard Perry during the Battle of Lake Erie, the Americans defeated the British Navy and by gaining control of Lake Erie, became a pivotal point of victory for the United States. Perry's Monument today stands 352 feet high and is an extremely popular tourist attraction for island goers of all ages. In addition, there are various wineries and watering holes and even the world's longest bar, the Beer Barrel Saloon, measuring in at 405 feet allowing for plenty of access for those looking for a cold one on those hot and muggy summer days.

During their days on the island before kids, Darian and Lisa would always visit the wineries with the assorted brands of cheese (Darian's favorite from the Cleveland Wine and Cheese after work parties), the Round House and of course the Beer Barrel Saloon. As Josh and then Taylor arrived, their trips became more family oriented with visits to the various caves, the wineries (with assorted juices for the kids) and of course, Perry's Monument.

The eighteen-minute ferry boat ride was coming to an end and Darian and Lisa commandeered the kids to take a hand as they disembarked off the boat onto the island. Passengers on foot always were the first to leave, then cyclists and finally the motorists. Since the Reillys planned on renting a golf cart they got off the boat right away, Darian secured one of the cart rental vendors and soon they were winging their way down Langram Road past the Put-In-Bay airport and into town.

The downtown area of Put-In-Bay was already bustling with shoppers, sightseers, cyclists and tourist shuttles. Darian had to employ the best of his road skills to navigate the tricky streets and all its weekend holiday clutter. By this time, it was almost 11:30 and Lisa suggested they grab an early lunch to beat the crowd.

"Excellent idea" said Darian since he had only his Saturday morning glass of juice and a banana to eat the entire morning.

As Langram Road turned left onto Toledo Avenue, the sight of the Boathouse Bar and Grille was too good to pass up. Darian pulled the golf cart around to the front, gave Lisa and the kids curbside service then made a fast left and parked on the corner of Toledo and Delaware Avenues.

As Lisa took Taylor to the restroom prior to being seated, Josh took advantage of the opportunity to see if he could win the favor of his dad.

"Any chance I can drive the golf cart, Dad?" the nine-year asked sheepishly.

Darian finally realized what he was up against. Josh had picked up some of his mother's habits, especially when he wanted something. Only instead of a foot rub, hair brushing or back massage like his mom, he wanted the keys to the car!

"We'll see", replied Darian, hoping against hope the distractions of the island would be enough to take Josh's mind off wanting to play cab driver the whole day.

The girls returned from the restroom, the family enjoyed a fabulous lunch consisting of club sandwiches, mac and cheese, salads and cheeseburgers. With a round of milkshakes and iced tea to wash everything down, the Reillys finished up, jumped into the cart and off to explore the island. Using the rare appearance of a local island police officer, Darian convinced Josh it would not be too smart for a nine-year old to be seen driving a golf cart while being spotted by a policeman. Although Josh did not like his father's decision, he understood and made the best of it. Later, his dad let him sit in his lap and steer as they drove through the less crowded streets on the island.

Since the line to Perry's Monument was relatively short due to the lunchtime crowd, they decided to head there first. As they walked inside to catch the elevator to the top, Darian and Lisa marveled at the history the monument represented. Even where they were standing was a place where several American and British soldiers who were killed during the Battle of Lake Erie had been buried.

"As a matter of fact, those soldiers are buried right beneath the exact spot where you're standing, young man" came the scratchy voice of the elderly monument tour guide.

Josh immediately looked down at the spot where he was standing as if waiting for something to jump right out of the floor. Darian and Lisa turned away with huge smiles and failed attempts to control their laughter while they admired the courage of their clearly spooked nine-year-old.

Finally, the elevator opened, Lisa took Taylor's hand and had to drag her away from all the written artifacts on the wall showing dates, times and places related to this part of our American history. When they arrived at the top, the view was spectacular. Since the humidity was low and the sky was clear, they could easily make out the edge of the Canadian coastline, less than 25 miles away. Middle Bass Island looked so close they could actually see people sitting on the deck of the Lonz Winery near the south end of the island. To the north a small single engine prop plane was coming in for a landing at Middle Bass Island Airport located on the far northern tip of the island, yet only a mile and a half away from Lonz. Middle Bass, unlike its big brother South Bass, was more a quieter, relaxing type of place where people could relax for the week and then boat over to Kelley's Island, Johnson's Island or even to the mainland.

"I never get tired of this view" Lisa said to her husband. "I still remember the first time you brought me here. I was so afraid of heights. That's why I held your hand" she confessed.

"Worked like a charm" Darian quipped. Lisa just shook her head and gave him that patented half smile.

The elevator arrived and in 90 seconds they were back on the ground headed for the safety of their golf cart. Josh kept looking back at the ground where he was standing above where the bodies of the soldiers were buried. And wondering....

Since they were on the historical part of their day, Darian drove the cart over to the entrance to the Perry Caves. Back during the War of 1812, the water on Lake Erie was full of bacteria and the men who drank it became violently ill and were unable to fight. The discovery of a cave on the island led to an underground spring of fresh water. The American soldiers were able to drink from the freshwater reservoir which enabled them to stay healthy and maintain control over the British fleet. Although unable to go deep into the cave to see the underground lake, there were plenty of pictures, graphics and writings about the entire freshwater phenomena. Naturally, Taylor had to be dragged away from the written descriptions of the historical events!

It wouldn't be a day at Put-In-Bay without stopping at one of the many wineries on the island. The Heineman Winery (nicknamed by locals as the Heine Winery) was Lisa's favorite and still had not changed its traditional look in over 40 years. By luck there was an empty table with four plastic chairs under one of the trees in the shade. Darian ordered a glass of wine for Lisa and himself and white grape juice for the kids. Since they had just finished lunch a few hours ago, he ordered a small plate of cheese sampler and much to his delight, no one else was interested in the mixed cheddar nuggets. Try as they might to keep the kids interested in the winery, the look of boredom soon shown across Josh' face. Noticing some of the happy hour locals were beginning to wander in, Darian and Lisa, communicating via a mutual non-verbal telepathic glance, decided maybe it was time to leave.

As it drew closer to dinner time the Reillys knew they had to make one more stop: The Beer Barrel Saloon. The four-hundred-foot bar in the saloon serpentined its way in and out of the building, sometimes out near the street where passersby could stop and relax and enjoy the view of the bay. Lisa got the kids each a root beer float while she and Darian sipped their water with lemon. A gentle breeze was blowing onto the bar area where they were seated, yet because the temperature was still in the 80s, it felt soothing and comfortable. After a few bowls of pretzels, the lemon waters and the root beer floats were gone. A few quick selfies while seated at the bar and the Reillys were off again.

Since it was Memorial Day weekend, the crowds around dinner time were extensive. Darian and Lisa decided to have dinner somewhere on the mainland and before the crazies of Put-In-Bay reared their ugly, alcoholic heads. Since they already purchased their return tickets on the ferry, there was no rush to get back. With Josh now firmly seated on his Dad's lap, he was able to steer the cart to the west and around the north end of the island. Although a little too early to catch that beautiful Lake Erie sunset, taking the scenic route back to ferry boat launch was as peaceful and exhilarating as one can imagine.

As the golf cart swung past the State Park and approached the entrance to the ferry boat launching dock, the Reillys couldn't help but notice a strange site. Two young boys, probably still in their teens, were performing a series of break dances, right out of the 1980s. As a crowd had started to collect around them, Darian and Lisa simply had to stop to look. Upon further review Darian discovered the boys had spent their ferry boat money on games, fun and souvenirs and forgot to set enough aside to buy return tickets on the ferry! "We're trying to break dance our way home" shouted one of the boys to no one in the crowd. Sure enough a small coffee can was sitting off to the side with a small collection of dollar bills. "Only on Put-In-Bay" Lisa laughed to Darian and the kids as she tucked a few singles into the can. Judging by the amount of bills nestled in the can, she determined the boys would be just fine.

The blast of the ferry boat horn was loud, indicating they were close to the boat launch. One thing about going to Put-In-Bay, you never had to glance at your watch. You knew by the sound of the Miller Boat Line that another twenty minutes had elapsed. Darian, with Josh's assistance, steered the golf cart into the return lot. All got out and meandered over to the pedestrian walkway which led onto the boat. Lisa took Taylor by the hand and the four of them were on the boat ready for the quick trip back to the mainland. Not nearly as crowded on the way back to Catawba as it had been earlier in the day, the Reillys nearly had the entire boat to themselves.

With the sound of the horn, they pulled away and were off, headed back to mainland. Standing near the bridge where the crew was sitting and enjoying the ride, Josh and Taylor kept getting curious looks from the captain as they began the short trip.

"Would you like to come up and see?" asked the captain.

The two youngsters were stunned.

"If it's ok with your mom and dad, come right in," added the captain as he glanced at Darian and Lisa.

"Go ahead kids. It's fine," their mom said with a smile.

Taylor was a little taken back but since her big brother was going to sit by the captain, she thought it was safe enough for her too. Josh was beside himself.

"This is amazing," the nine-year old shouted over the roar of the load engines. "Dad, this is so cool." The excitement of being near the captain on the trip home made it seem even shorter for the young boy.

A few minutes later, the horn sounded, the boat's engines propelled them into a slow, steady crawl into the docking site and the passengers started to head for the lower level. As the two children started to head back to their parents, they heard their mother's familiar voice.

"What did we forget" questioned Lisa as she stared at her two youngsters.

"Thank you" the two children bellowed out to the Captain almost in unison.

"You're very welcome kids, came the Captain's reply. You both did a great job steering the boat back safely" he chuckled with a grin.

Darian thanked the captain for the wonderful treat of letting his kids sit on the bridge and turned to leave. Taylor took her dad's hand and headed down the steep metal steps to the lower level. Josh couldn't believe his luck. Having been able to drive a golf cart and steer a ferry boat all in one day. Not nearly enough lemon juice around to wipe that smile off his face!

As the family made their way off the boat and over to the parking lot, they all seemed to come to the same, unanimous realization: They were hungry. Since Catawba was more of a residential area, they decided to stop in neighboring Port Clinton where the choices for dinner were far more plentiful. After passing the more common eateries, they decided to pull into Dock's Beach House and Restaurant situated right on the water. The sun was setting over the edge of Lake Erie creating a wonderful atmosphere prior to the hour-long drive back to Bay Village. By the time they had finished their dinner night had already fallen and the remainder of the trip would be in the dark.

"However, Darian whispered to Lisa, it's never too late for a fudge and/or ice cream stop, correct"?

Lisa concurred, allowing her husband and children one last indulgence to cap off the first unofficial day of summer. A quick stop on the way over to Jolly Roger's Seafood House was just the thing. Not only seafood but they had the best chocolate fudge, ice cream and taffy to satisfy the weariest of travelers.

Finally, after the seafood, the fudge and the taffy had been consumed, the Reillys piled into the Suburban and began the hour-long drive back home. By this time darkness had set in and the family was headed east on Route 2 first through Huron, then Lorain and finally to Westlake. They pulled off I-90 and headed north onto Crocker-Bassett Rd just before 10:30 pm. As Darian turned right onto Lake Road, he noticed both kids were sound asleep. Even pulling into the brightly lit garage didn't seem to wake them. Lisa picked up Taylor and carried her up to bed while Darian helped Josh stagger out of the car in a semi-conscious state and into his dad's waiting arms. Exhausted from the long day and the drive home, after putting the kids down for the night, Darian and Lisa crawled into bed, flipped on the TV and were out within minutes.

May 29

The incessant licking of the Reilly's dog, Neely, awakened Darian from a sound, dream filled sleep. It was not quite 8am and Neely always knew when it was Sunday, the day when she and her master took their regularly scheduled walk down Lake Road to Huntington Beach. Lisa, lying motionless on her side of the bed didn't even stir as Darian quickly got up, petted the Irish Setter and chased her down to the kitchen and out the door. Rescued as a pup from the local dog pound on Willey Ave, Neely was ever so obedient as well as playful while at the same time very protective of Lisa, Josh and Taylor. Once when Lisa was out walking by herself and the kids, they were approached by a stranger looking for directions. Neely barked continuously until the man thanked Lisa and was a comfortable distance away. Darian always knew if he were ever out of town, Neely would make sure to sound the alarm in the event an unwanted intruder came near the house.

By the time Darian had returned from their walk Lisa was already up and greeted him in the kitchen. By now it was almost mid-morning and cereal, bananas and milk cluttered the breakfast table. Josh and Taylor, fresh from a good night's sleep, had already dug in while Darian filled Neely's food and water bowl. With the WKYC news and weather in the background, another perfect weather day was promised to Northeastern Ohio. And what a day it was going to be. Darian's racquetball partner and good friend Jack Flynn, along with his wife Anna and their three children, invited the Reillys to spend the day on Jack's 32-foot Sea Ray power boat, *Social Distance.*

Jack and Darian had met at the University of Michigan as undergraduates years earlier. Although the two had talked about working together in some sort of a business venture someday, Jack had decided to attend law school at the Cleveland Marshall College of Law and later took a job with the law firm of McDonald, Hopkins and Hardy in downtown Cleveland after graduating. The concept of being a Michigan graduate living in Northern Ohio among thousands of Ohio State fans seemed to force Jack and Darian to form a sort of "us against the world" special bond. Despite the playful teasing they received from the many OSU faithful, they still laughed it off and never were shy about their allegiance to *That Team Up North.*

Anna had met Jack when he was still in law school as she worked as a registered nurse in the emergency room at Lakewood Hospital. When this tall, thinly built softball player wandered into the ER with a wrist the size of a cantaloupe, she had an exceedingly difficult time taking her eyes off him. Like Darian, Jack loved sports and was ultra-competitive. That night, after a diving attempt in vain of catching a sharply hit line drive resulting in a fractured wrist, nurse Anna took command of the injured player in Treatment Room 8. "It's a fractured ulna, she told him as he glanced at the X-ray film. "What's an ulna," replied Jack rather shighly. "It's one of the two bones you have in your arm which connects to your hand." she exclaimed. "Why do they call it an ulna, he queried. "That would take too long to explain, she replied. "Then maybe over dinner you could explain it to me" he stammered with a smile.

One wedding, a mortgage and three kids later, the Flynns were situated as neighbors and best friends of the Reillys in Bay Village. Jack had already texted Darian to meet at Eddy's Boat Dock in Rocky River at 11am. Since it was fast approaching 10 already, Lisa instructed Josh and Taylor to finish their breakfast and tidy up their rooms before they left to go boating for the day. Darian sent a text over to Paul thanking him for taking care of Neely the day before and providing further instructions to look in on her as the Reillys would be gone most of the day. Lisa was putting the finishing touches on the cooler they were bringing which included drinks, snacks and treats for the kids and adults. Darian made sure all the windows in the house were closed and secure. One never knows when one of those Canadian fronts can blow through, causing a sudden storm off the lake, he reasoned to himself. Living near the lake certainly had its advantages, however, on a few occasions the neighborhood electrical power had fallen victim to mother nature.

Darian grabbed the cooler; Lisa brought an abundance of towels and sunblock and Josh and Taylor jumped into the back seat of the Suburban. Since the Flynn's boat was wet docked in Rocky River only a few miles away, it was a short ride down Lake Road briefly through the Wooster Rd entrance to the Metro Park and a right turn into Eddy's.

The Cleveland Metro Park was a forty-four-mile collection of woods, hiker biker trails, horse trails and ball fields surrounding the city. Nicknamed "The Emerald Necklace" because of its appearance of a green necklace around the city of Cleveland from the air, it is a great source of fishing, bird watching and recreation in the summer and sledding, tobogganing and cross-country skiing in the winter. The Rocky River, located on the west side of Cleveland, is a tremendous source of fishing and boating leading directly into the waiting arms of Lake Erie. Once a boater leaves any of the assorted marinas on the river, they are conveniently only a few minutes from the downtown area while passing beautiful views of the Lakewood Gold Coast and the approaching Cleveland skyline. An excellent spot to park a 28-foot Sea Ray.

The Flynns young son Matthew, was a year older than Josh but played with him frequently. Their two girls, Sarah and Katy were friends with Taylor as well. Sarah was the same age as Taylor and both girls attended the same summer camp. Katy was a year younger and just graduated from kindergarten at Normandy. The kids were all excited about spending the day on the boat. Matthew took charge of making sure his two sisters had their life jackets secured then handed one each to Josh and Taylor. Lisa and Anna took seats with the girls near the back of the boat while Matthew and Josh sat up front in the bow rider. Within minutes the Sea Ray was backing out of its dock space with Jack at the controls and slowly navigated north up the river through the assorted no wake zones. Passing under the Clifton Boulevard bridge, the open waters of Lake Erie lay ahead.

"Everyone hold on," yelled Jack as he reached down to increase the throttle.

With a mild jolt they were off the calm waters of the river and headed out to the open sea. Although the Sea Ray's 300 horsepower engine could easily reach 60 miles per hour, Jack held it steady at 35 along the relatively calm lake surface. Even though the Memorial Day weather was comfortable, the lake water usually takes a few more weeks to warm up to the point of partaking in activities such as tubing, swimming and water skiing. Even the occasional spray over the bow this time of year can provide a chilling reminder that just two months ago, there was *ice* on this lake. Matthew and Josh quickly discovered this as they tried to shield themselves from the intermittent cold splashes.

Heading east past the old Sheppard Bay View Hospital, now the Cashelmara Condominiums, the Lakewood Gold Coast and Edgewater Beach, they finally arrived at the northernmost end of the Cuyahoga river where it dumps into Lake Erie in downtown Cleveland. The sight of all the assorted restaurants along both sides of the river did not go unnoticed.

"I'm hungry," Darian announced to no one hoping that the other three adults would pick up the hint.

"Didn't Lisa tell you?" asked Jack. "You can eat as much as you can catch today," he laughed referring to the abundance of bass and carp fishing which Lake Erie was famous for.

Darian was never much of a fisherman. The thought of sitting for hours trying to catch a fish just didn't seem to have much appeal. "Thanks, but as much fun as that sounds, I'll take D'Poos on the River or the Flat Iron Cafe, thank you," he joked.

As Jack commandeered the Sea Ray past the Nautica outdoor concert park on the west side of the river, Lisa and Anna both spotted the Brick and Barrel Restaurant and with its kid friendly outdoor seating, was too good to pass up. Darian jumped up front to the bow to help Jack guide the boat safely over to one of the nearby docking areas. Once secured, the kids unbuckled their life jackets and all took a parent's hand as they walked up the small boardwalk to the restaurant. Darian quickly commandeered a large table right near the water but with plenty of shade from the overhang for all nine of them. The kids dined on an assortment of chicken fingers, PB&J and mac and cheese while the four adults kept to their end of the table and discussed various social topics while consuming cheeseburgers and salads. Though they loved having a few cold beers on this summer afternoon, Jack and Darian were very cognizant of the laws of boating and alcohol and simply ordered diet cokes and water to avoid any trouble the rest of the afternoon.

While the women chatted about the assorted neighborhood gossip, the men turned their conversation to sports and yard work. It was always an unwritten rule that the two friends rarely broached the subject about work unless it directly involved them both. With the Central Division first place Indians looking like they might make another World Series run, the Cavs just coming off an NBA World Championship and the Browns showing their usual off-season promise, there was plenty to talk about.

After lunch, the two families headed for the boat, did a safety check to make sure all had their life jackets and after a slow and steady short trip north up the Cuyahoga river, headed out to an open and welcoming Lake Erie. Jack hit the throttle and headed east first passing First Energy Stadium which the Browns called home, then the Rock and Roll Hall of Fame and finally passing Burke Lakefront Airport. The rest of the afternoon was spent out near Mentor Headlands Beach and then a quick tour north to the infamous Five Mile Crib, a water intake station located five miles off the coast of downtown Cleveland. The Crib always served as a great spot to enjoy a panoramic view of the North Coast and on a clear day, one could see all the way to Canada to the north. Despite the relative cool water temperature, the boys were still anxious to get some tubing in along with their younger sisters.

On days like these no one ever keeps an eye on the time. As the sun started to set the adults decided that perhaps it was time to turn for home. Rather than head back down the Cuyahoga and try to battle the Memorial Day crowds for dinner, an executive decision was made to head west and chase the sun back to the boat dock and grab a bite closer to home. By the time they had reached Rocky River everyone was a bit hungry and just a little wiped from the day's activities. Jack steadily navigated the Sea Ray back into the no wake zone on the river.

The kids all unbuckled their life jackets and stored them neatly in the box at the rear of the boat. Lisa and Anna were busy picking up what was left of towels, drinks and snacks. Jack and Darian were busy tying down the boat and bumpers making it safe and secure until the next outing.

"See you at Herb's" proclaimed Jack as he, Anna and the kids pulled away in their GMC Yukon.

"Right behind you" replied Darian as Lisa, Josh and Taylor jumped into the Suburban.

Herb's Tavern was an age-old joint located near the border of Lakewood and Rocky River on Detroit Rd. and Herburgers were famous all over town. Herb Anderson, the original owner, had died unexpectedly of a heart attack years ago and his two sons were now running the place. One of the traditions of eating at Herb's was that he *always* had the television on. Some say it was because he loved the Indians and simply had to have every game on. Others say it was because it gave the place more of a home type atmosphere. In any case, the Flynns, arriving first, were able to uncharacteristically grab a table which seated both them and the Reillys. Both families, although a bit wiped from a long day of boating, were equally hungry and the evening commenced to the tune of burgers, fries, mac and cheese soft drinks and draft beer.

As the waitress brought the check to the table, Darian snatched it up, much to Jack's chagrin.

"No way, no way, dude" Jack exclaimed. "We're splittin' that mate" he said.

"Please" Lisa interjected. This was such a great time today; it's the least we can do".

"Well thanks just the same, Jack replied. And anytime you want to take it out you know you are welcome to do so".

Darian just smiled back, and the two exhausted families headed for home. It was nearly 11 pm by the time the Reillys arrived home with the kids. All were exhausted and everyone was asleep the moment their heads hit the pillow. Tomorrow was Memorial Day, a day the family could relax.

May 30

The endless supply of Neely's kisses woke Darian from a deep and much needed slumber as the morning of Memorial Day dawned. Realizing her dad was home from work meant only one thing to this rather intelligent canine: This was the day we take our walk along the beach and chase the geese. Darian, forcing his eyes to come to grips with the fast-fading hope that his dog's need for attention was only a dream, glanced at his iPhone and saw "7:12 Monday May 30".

"Ok" he whispered to Neely hoping she would keep it quiet so Lisa and the kids would not be disturbed. Darian marched his dog downstairs to the kitchen, filled her bowl and refreshed her water. While Neely was enjoying her breakfast, Darian jumped into his running shoes, grabbed a quick cup of juice and headed out the door with Neely on a leash. Because the Reillys lived only a short distance from the Lake, the morning air was slightly brisker than most of the community. Heading east on Lake Rd, noticing an increasing number of tear down houses on the northern lake side, Darian couldn't help but think if perhaps someday, he and Lisa might be entertaining grandchildren at their house on the lake. Passing by the old Dr. Sam house just a few doors down from Huntington Beach, he and Neely made their way down the hundred or so concrete steps to the beach below.

Suddenly he felt a jerk from the leash. It seemed Neely had a strong desire to run and chase after something. Since they pretty much had the beach to themselves, keeping with their weekend tradition, let Neely run free. "Neels", he shouted. The Irish Setter came to an abrupt halt and waited for her master to catch up. Darian petted the dog repeatedly then threw a stick which she retrieved after advancing more than fifteen yards into the Lake Erie waters. A rare weekend moment when Darian found himself alone and time to think, he started to wonder about the issues and potential troubles at DigiNet. Things are never as good as they seem or as bad as they seem, one of his mentors, James Sheppard once told him.

But try as he might, Darian was unable to shake DigiNet and its financial troubles from his mind. Even while watching the beautiful Lake Erie Sunset from the Flynn's boat the night before, Darian's mind kept wandering off to the offices of TRW, Cleveland Health Alliance and Ed Blackwell. Even Jack could tell something was up when Darian refused to take the wheel of the vessel. Although he loved boating and the water, Darian knew a $60,000 toy was something he just could not afford for a while. Somehow the peaceful view of the sunrise on the eastern edge of Lake Erie made Darian realize that things will be ok and to stop and enjoy the view and his family.

After an hour long walk along the beach, Darian arrived home to find Lisa in the kitchen, but the kids were still asleep.

"We are almost out of cereal and we need a few things for lunch", Lisa said as she gave Darian a kiss. I am going to make a trip to Giant Eagle and have a list together. Is there anything you need, honey" she asked?

"No" Darian replied in a short, swift tone.

"Are you alright?", Lisa inquired as she wondered why her husband suddenly snapped at her.

"Yes, I'm sorry, honey." he responded. "You know how I get when I have an empty stomach".

"Do you want me to fix you some eggs?" she asked.

"No, it's ok. I can do it. You go on ahead to the grocery. Do you need me to come along?" he asked.

"No, I'm just getting a few things for today and the rest of the week. I'll see you soon. Love you!" Lisa said as she headed out the door.

"Maybe a pizza night" Darian shouted to her as she was backing out of the driveway, but his words fell on deaf ears.

Darian knew he needed to just relax. Everything at DigiNet would work itself out. Today was going to be a beautiful day with his wife and kids and he wasn't about to let some preconceived thoughts about his business affairs get in the way of that. As Josh and Taylor made their way down to the kitchen, Darian got them their juice and cereal and talked about what they might do today. "I've got some grass to cut and some yard work to do but maybe afterwards you and Mom and I can all take our bikes and ride over to Cahoon park on the trails. "Or maybe the Metro Park" Josh perked up. "That's certainly a possibility," Darian replied. Let's all get our chores done first since we've been away for the past two days and then we'll talk to mom when she gets home.

Josh and Taylor were no slouches when it came to being outdoors. They both loved their sports, as well as biking and swimming during the summer. Maybe because the long, harsh winters in Northern Ohio kept them indoors it seemed for months at a time. But Darian and Lisa would like to think that their kids took after their own active mom and dad who always seemed to be on the go.

Lisa arrived home with a mountain of groceries. Josh and Taylor stopped their chores to help her cart them into the kitchen. Darian, meanwhile, had taken to the lawnmower to get a jump on his 'to-do" list, hoping to salvage a portion of the afternoon and early evening with Lisa and the kids.

By midafternoon, the entire family was congregated in the garage. Darian was going through a final tune-up on everyone's bikes, making sure the tires were adequately inflated and the brakes and gears worked. Everyone donned their helmets and the Reillys were headed over to Cahoon Park in the center of Bay Village.

Joseph Cahoon and his family had settled in the area back in 1810. Upon the death of the last member of the Cahoon family, near the turn of the 20th century, the land which belonged to the Cahoon family was donated to the city of Bay Village. But there was one condition: The park was not to be used on Sundays as that was a day for church, family and home, so the legend goes. Since today was a Monday, the park was buzzing with baseball games, tennis, joggers and families with bikes and strollers.

Bay Village was once a sleepy little cottage town and at one time served as a makeshift vacation spot for Clevelanders during the early 1900s. By 1950 it had become its own municipality. Although the growth of the Greater Cleveland area included much to the west and southwest of the city, unlike its neighbors, Westlake, Avon and North Olmsted which sported several industrial and business pockets, it seemed Bay Village was able to maintain a residential feel throughout the entire community. It was this down home and residential feel which attracted the Reillys to this fashionable suburb. It almost seemed as if everyone in town knew each other, or at least behaved that way toward each other.

Lisa led the pack toward the trails off the central portion of the park and headed south toward the old R&R railroad which had since become a popular hiker biker trail. Josh followed his mom with Taylor closely behind him. Darian brought up the rear to keep an eye on his six-year-old daughter who was still a novice at two-wheel bike riding. The family had planned to make this a relatively short outing since it was still a school night but like the many canoe trips down the Rocky River, they seemed to get caught up in the moment.

Before they knew it, the time was approaching almost 5pm. The family had biked on and off for the past two hours and the kids were starting to get hungry.

"How about we take the shortcut home and then we order some pizza", Lisa queried.

A huge, unanimous yes came from her kids and husband. Without saying a word, Lisa turned north off the main trail and headed along the old Bassett Rd. trail which would get them home in the next twenty minutes. They liked the Bassett Rd trail because the road was in the

Guinness Book of World records as the only road in the country in which one could travel in all four directions headed the same way. The trail mirrored the road and of course, Taylor kept track of which directions they had already covered, and which ones were yet to come.

As they arrived home, the kids nestled their bikes next to Darian's. Lisa, requesting valet service from her husband, left him to parking detail and galloped into the house.

"Where will you be when your diarrhea comes back?" he joked to the kids.

"I heard that!" Lisa shouted from inside the house.

Pizza, drinks and ice cream capped out the day as the Reillys listened to some holiday fireworks being shot off in the distance. Tomorrow was Tuesday and back to work. Darian was wondering what fireworks lay ahead for him at DigiNet.

June 6

Not only was he getting more and more nervous about the company's financial situation, but Darian was also getting annoyed that his calls and messages to TRW were not being returned. He had a few other smaller security firm deals in the mix but they were short term projects, usually over in a 2–3-week period. He really needed a flagship deal like TRW to not only put DigiNet on the map but keep them alive. Jack Flynn had texted asking if they could move their Wednesday racquetball day to Tuesday of this week. He had to fly to Dallas on business on Wednesday and would not be available. Sure, no problem replied Darian. That will free up the rest of his week in case the TRW deal comes through, he reasoned.

Darian loved athletics and competition and the individual sports such as golf and racquetball filled this niche quite well. He and Jack were both 'A' players on the court and were evenly matched. Every Wednesday afternoon they had a regularly scheduled match at River Oaks Racquet Club in nearby Rocky River. This particular day Darian took the first game but lost to Jack on a come from behind victory which frustrated Darian a bit. There was always a little bit of friendly competition between the two friends and winning the first two out of three would have been a minor victory, something Darian sorely needed these days.

Jack came storming back in game three and trounced Darian 21-9.

"I could tell your mind was somewhere else" Jack conveyed to Darian.

"Forget it," he snapped. Let's go get a cold one since it's on me."

Without showering the two went to the lounge and ordered a couple drafts. Darian thanked Jack again for the holiday boat ride.

"Someday I would love to have one of those myself" he said referring to Jack's Sea Ray.

"Anytime you feel comfortable with it you are welcome to take it out" replied Jack.

A nice gesture but Darian knew it was not going to happen. He signed the bill and both men headed for the shower and back to work. As Jack and Darian were walking out, Renee, who worked behind the bar, asked Darian for his credit card. Apparently the one the club had on file was declined. When she tried to run it a second time it was declined again.

"Computer glitch" said Jack. "Put it on my account" he commanded Renee who took care of it.

"Thanks buddy" said Darian as they walked away. "Not sure what happened there but I owe you one."

"Think nothing of it dude" said Jack. "See you in a week."

As Darian sat alone in his Audi still in the River Oaks parking lot, he couldn't help but wonder. On the drive back to the office he called Society Bank and asked to speak to Ted Christian who had become his personal banker over the last several years. Ted was out on appointments that day but Ellie, his administrative assistant got on the phone with Darian.

"The bank has reduced your line of credit on this account", she said. "That may be the reason why it was declined", she said.

"Would you have Mr. Christian call me as soon as possible please?" he barked over the phone to Ellie.

The Reillys had been with Society Bank for eleven years. Darian was a little put off that he didn't even receive a text or email from his personal banker about this reduction of credit.

Upon returning to the office, he asked Lori if all the bills were paid on time. She said they were, but their cash reserves were at a six-month low, not a good sign.

"Is everything alright?" she asked. But Darian walked back to his office without saying a word. The company had been through some tough times before but needed an infusion of cash. If something didn't happen soon DigiNet would be in serious trouble.

Lisa had just sent her last email to a group of moms who were interested in summer camp for their kids. Most of them had kids the same ages as Josh and Taylor which made it very convenient to plan the events.

Lisa was meticulous with her emails. Each one had to be absolutely perfect before she hit the 'send' button. Sometimes she would read them aloud before approving the final draft. Upon sending out this last email to all the moms, she realized she had nothing planned for dinner. It was 5 pm so she commanded Josh and Taylor to jump in the car so they could get to the grocery store before their dad got home. Lisa couldn't grille but she was great at salads and desserts. She picked up some items from produce and the meat section then let the kids run everything through the self-serve checkout. Naturally, Taylor had to read the label on each item scanned!

When she inserted her credit card into the machine, she noticed it came back declined. That's funny, she thought. She and Darian were victims of credit card fraud a few months back, so she assumed it was their bank being cautious again. Luckily, she had enough cash to cover the grocery bill.

Just then a text message arrived from Darian:

Running a little late. Home by 6.

Lisa sent a quick reply:

NP   Leaving Giant Eagle now.   Card declined   more bank fraud???

"Great", Darian thought to himself. "Now our personal credit is getting affected."

Lisa and the kids made it home by 5:30. Taylor did her best to help her mom prepare the tossed salad while Lisa put the finishing touches on a generous batch of marinated chicken. Corn on the cob also helped save the day. Josh was in the driveway shooting baskets when he saw his dad's Audi make its way down meandering Inglewood Drive. Maybe a bit competitive like Darian, Josh was determined to hit this last shot before his dad's arrival and nailed a fifteen-footer as he stepped out of the way to see his dad pull into the driveway, just before 6pm. Listening to the local sports talk station on the way home Darian learned the Indians were still leading the Central Division by 3 ½ games over the Minnesota Twins. The Tribe started a three-game series on the road against the last place Boston Red Sox. The thought of increasing their Central Division lead and dinner with Lisa and the kids on the patio brightened the young entrepreneur's mood immeasurably.

June 8

Arriving to work just a little before 7:30 the next morning, Darian was determined to see what the story was with TRW. The meeting with Bob Clifford and Bill Hegarty had gone very well, or so he thought. Clearly their company had security and IT issues but was it evident to them that DigiNet could do the job? Darian's company enjoyed a solid reputation of quality work and great customer support. If TRW were to realize this as well, then his worries were over.

However, DigiNet only had a few other proposals in the hopper, one of which was with the US Government Dept of Homeland Security. Darian didn't pay much attention to that one because not only was it a long shot, but it wouldn't take effect until October when the government started its new fiscal year. By getting to the office before anyone had arrived, he logged on to his DigiNet email. Nothing so far but it was still only 7am. Noticing a few of the routine bills were shortly due to be paid, Darian took a moment to glance at the bills he pays at home. His credit cards were behind and now the water and electric were lagging as well. Funny thing about utility bills like water and electric. While they do not affect your credit directly, they tend to just shut your service off if you do not pay the bill. Darian knew something had to be done and fast. Both cars were now close to thirty days behind and shortly calls from creditors will begin. He and Lisa always had great credit, so he was bound and determined to do whatever it took to maintain their good standing.

Suddenly in his inbox there was an email from Bob Clifford with the words "TRW Proposal" in the subject line. Finally, he was going to be able to get things back to normal financially both at work and at home, he thought. Finally, he could enjoy a good night's sleep without waking up at 3:30 am thinking about it. Finally, he wouldn't have those embarrassing moments for Lisa at the grocery store or with Jack at River Oaks racquet club. He clicked on the email and could not believe his eyes….

Darian,

Thank you for taking the time with Bill Hegarty and myself to go over your plan to help us overcome our security and IT issues here at TRW.

Regretfully, we have decided to move forward with another company which we felt is better suited in helping us with the concerns we have.

Please know that we still highly value the merits of your company and will not hesitate to contact you should we require your services in the future.

Best regards,

Robert H. Clifford

Chief Operating Officer

TRW Corporation

Darian was stunned. TRW decided to enter into a contract with Media Trex! He knew that TRW had whittled it down to them and DigiNet. Although Media Trex was a much larger company than DigiNet, they had the reputation of providing extremely poor customer support, something Gerry and Darian hammered home during their meeting. Since Clifford had stressed the importance of support and follow up and expressed a specific desire to work with more local companies, Darian thought for sure the contract would be theirs.

He seemed to be gasping for air as he was having difficulty breathing. He couldn't believe what he had just absorbed. He read it over and over. He glanced at his watch. It was 7:38 am. The rest of the company was due to arrive in just a few minutes. He knew Lisa was driving the kids to Normandy at this very moment. It seemed like he had nowhere to turn. He had to think clearly and move fast.

Suddenly there was a knock on the office door. Gerry poked his head halfway into Darian's office and couldn't help but notice the dejected look on his boss' face.

"Media Trex?" he asked. Without even meeting Gerry's glance, Darian just nodded haphazardly as he continued to stare at his laptop without uttering a word. "They do this. They are such great pitchmen and then the customer comes crying to us months later hoping someone will come in and clean up the mess" Gerry shouted. "Don't these companies ever perform any due diligence?" he thundered. "Don't they know about the horrible job they did with Cleveland State and Lorain County and Price Waterhouse? These guys are a fucking joke. And they know we can do this job at a fraction…."

Darian raised his hand signaling to his associate that what's done is done and for the moment they have to stay calm and think this through.

Gerry marched over to his office and sat down at his desk, staring at the wall in disgust. His presentation to Bob Clifford and Bill Hegarty could not have been better. Had he missed something? Did he piss them off? Were they simply trying to get information on how DigiNet operated knowing they would never make a deal? These random thoughts raced through Gerry's analytical mind. It was 7:49 am and the rest of the office staff was due to arrive within minutes.

Although DigiNet was Darian's creation, Gerry was the first person he brought on when the company was formed. A tall, fiery individual by nature, Gerry had that rare talent to stay calm and composed when the situation called for it. Although not much of an athlete in high school or college, Gerry was the intellectual who could always decipher the code or overcome an internet obstacle or fix a computer glitch.

Growing up on the west side of Cleveland, Gerry Finn was the youngest of three children. After his father died when he was eleven, Gerry's mother went back to work as a preschool teacher and supplemented their income working at Sweetbriar Golf Course during the summers to help make ends meet. For most of his grade school and high school years, he was left to figure things out on his own. His brother James and his sister Kathleen were seven and nine years older, respectively. By the time Gerry had graduated from St. Coleman's in the 8th grade, his brother and sister had moved on to college and seemed to lose touch with their youngest sibling. Gerry's mother always tried to make time for her son but the demands of working two jobs made it exceedingly difficult to be home for him much of the time.

Gerry would immerse himself in books, instructional videos and how to fix-it-manuals. He had a constant interest in gadgets and electronics. If there was something new on the market, Gerry was the first to get it and try it out. If there were an old technology that seemed outdated, Gerry would always be the one to try and modernize it. Indeed, at age 13 he had been given an old 18th Century Italian Flintlock Pistol by his grandfather and without regard to the gun's possible net worth, attempted to design and reverse engineer a silencer just to see if he could!

It was at a summer science fair at Case Western Reserve University where he ran into a person at one of the IT booths and struck up a conversation. After going back and forth about the various ways to breach the ins and outs of IT and internet security with this person, he quickly surmised that the two had quite a bit in common. "I just started my own company", the newcomer said. "And I'm looking for someone who has the technical know-how to help me over the rough spots when it comes to tech support." After a lengthy discussion on how to market this type of support, Gerry and his new out of town friend, Darian Reilly, became lifelong friends and business associates.

But now the two mates had to put their collective heads together and figure out how to remedy the sinking ship. Although Gerry was not as business savvy as Darian, he still understood the gravity of the situation.

He knew DigiNet was not a huge company and losing the TRW deal only made things geometrically worse.

"I heard that the Westlake Porter Library was in need of some updating with their feedback loops and their fault tolerant systems," Gerry offered. They don't require assessments and their system is way outdated. Their administrator is Bridget Mahoney who lives five minutes away from our farm. I'll call her and see if we can set something up."

"Thanks." Darian nodded with a half-smile as he turned his attention back to the matters at hand.

He knew that June, July and August were prime vacation months for many who braved the harsh Cleveland winters and arranging meetings with customers can be difficult during this time. He and Lisa and the kids were scheduled to leave for their own annual summer weeklong vacation down to Myrtle Beach next week and now Darian wondered if there would even be a DigiNet to come back to when they got back....

June 12

The month of June in Cleveland had always promised to have warm temperatures and the excitement of a fun filled summer which lie ahead. Kids were out of school, outdoor sports and activities were in high gear and summer vacations were off and running. And the Reillys were no exception. Each year the Reilly's vacationed down to Myrtle Beach, South Carolina almost always staying at the same condo. The thought of relaxing and laying on the beach or by the pool for an entire week always gave them something to look forward to during the long, harsh winter months. Josh was just a baby when they made their first trip. Lisa was always capturing everything on camera while Darian operated the video cam. They even recognized numerous people who had also made the trip from Ohio. It was going to be a long ten-hour drive, so Lisa made sure there were plenty of snacks, books and movies for the kids to watch.

Lisa had the kids pack their things for the trip. Taylor, of course brought along plenty of reading material while Josh made sure all his portable electronic games were packed and ready. In years past the Reillys would have to load up on car seats, strollers and assorted baby items. As the kids were now growing older, packing up the Suburban became a much simpler task. In the past they would pack their bikes because Taylor was too young to ride on a rental but this year, she was excited to ride her very own big girl bike. Renting bikes for the family now saved Darian much needed time and convenience.

"If we leave by 7am we should comfortably be there by 5," Lisa said to Darian.

"Roger that," he replied. I'll grab the neighborhood car top carrier and make sure we are loaded up tonight and ready to go."

Years ago, the Reillys, along with several of the neighbors, got together and collectively purchased a 24,000 cubic inch hard shell car top carrier. Since the cost was split among several neighborhood families, it easily paid for itself in one summer. Each year, Darian would send out an online calendar allowing each family to pick a time to reserve the carrier. Many times throughout the year neighbors would be sharing everything from tools to snow blowers to babysitters. Since everyone took vacations at different times, sharing a community car top carrier made perfect sense.

June 13

That morning, promptly at 7am, the Reillys jumped into their Suburban and began the ten-hour trek toward the South Carolina coast. Darian was trying to be calm about their finances, but he wondered how any of this would affect them while on vacation. Would their credit cards still work? Would they be able to withdraw cash from an ATM? What if they had car trouble? All these things kept going through his mind as he steered the car southbound on Interstate 77 toward the southern Ohio border. Should he tell Lisa? He was always up front with her and he knew she was a good sounding board for him. He decided he was not going to ruin her and the kids' vacation. He would tell her when they got home at the end of the week.

Perhaps the warmth of the sun or the play on the beach or just being with his wife and kids was the reason. But something made him forget about the seriousness of their situation and just enjoy the week away from everything and everyone. The Reillys made sandcastles, rode bikes on the beach, surfed the five-foot Carolina waves on their boogie boards and enjoyed some excellent seafood, particularly lobster and crab, Lisa's favorite.

As luck would have it, the remnants of Hurricane Christine showed off its remaining muscle creating abnormal eight-to-nine-foot waves for the tourists to enjoy. Josh was easily tossed by the commanding sea and hardly made it out past a few yards offshore. Darian, perhaps still trying to impress his wife with his Beach Boy Dennis Wilson wannabe surfing skills, attempted in vain to stay up on his board for only a few seconds. Since the condo they had rented had both an outdoor pool and easy access to the beach, the Reillys were able to toggle back and forth when deciding which form of water entertainment they preferred. And because Darian was an early riser, he frequently would be up to catch the morning sunrise off the eastern Carolina coast. Usually by the time he returned to the condo Lisa was up sipping her morning coffee seated on the balcony overlooking the beach.

One morning, the temperature had risen into the upper 80s, but Darian had made it a point to get in his morning jog regardless. As Lisa spotted her husband slowly coming up the concrete walkway toward her, she raised her coffee as if to ask, "can I pour you a cup?" Darian, drenched in sweat from the ungodly heat and humidity, shouted "water" to her. Knowing her husband as well as she did, she tossed a bottle of smart water which she had ready for him into the hands of the desperate, dehydrated man.

But as always, the weeklong vacation came and went so swiftly and soon their Chevy Suburban was pointed northbound toward home. All the easiness Darian had enjoyed this past week was a distant memory and he was forced to confront the financial pitfalls which lay ahead. After stopping at a roadside restaurant in West Virginia, he went to pay for the lunch. When the card was declined, he was getting frustrated. He paid the $36 in cash without Lisa knowing, as she and Taylor had gone to the restroom before they commenced on their trip home. Calls on his cell phone were coming in more and more frequently from banks and credit card companies wanting to collect overdue payments. Things were getting out of control. When he got in the car, Darian simply shut off his iPhone completely.

The winding drive north on I-77 was picturesque and scenic, to say the least. The view of some portions of the Appalachian Mountains were breathtaking. Lisa was snapping pictures on the way home to capture the moment. As they passed a sign which said "Whitewater Rafting" near Ohio Pyle State Park in West Virginia it reminded her of the times she and Darian, along with a group of several of their friends, had made the trip for a weekend of rafting, fun and downright partying. Thoughts of their adventures from years past on the Cheat, the New and the Youghiogheny Rivers made her put down her camera and nudge her husband.

"Wasn't it the 'Yak' that was the most treacherous?" she asked referring to the dangerous Youghiogheny River. "Wasn't that the time we had a guide in the boat that had warned us about 'Pinball Rock?'" she continued. "Darian" she pleaded. "Are you listening?"

"Yes, yes, I'm sorry" he replied as he came back to reality. "Pinball Rock. Yes, I do remember that" he stammered trying to keep his attention on the road while thinking about DigiNet while at the same time trying to respond to Lisa.

"What is it, honey," she asked him. I can always tell when there is something wrong." Darian half smiled at his beautiful, but ever so in tune wife, who at times seemed to be able to read his thoughts.

"Just a little post vacation blues" he added hoping this would satisfy his wife's line of questioning.

"I know. It was such a great time. Maybe we should go down next year with Jack and Anna and their kids" she remarked. The thought of how successful Jack Flynn had been since their college days and now with Darian staring down the barrel of his company going belly up certainly did not help to hide his sense of uneasiness.

Finally, the Suburban crossed the Ohio border which was good for two reasons. One, it was a much flatter drive and two they were only two and a half hours from home. By the time they had reached Cuyahoga County everyone was getting hungry. Lisa called ahead to order Chipotle which made it easy for them to drive by and just pick up the food about a mile from home. By the time they had pulled into their driveway it was almost 9pm and everyone was exhausted. The kids jumped out of the car and headed for the kitchen table. Lisa grabbed the food while Darian grabbed a few pieces of luggage.

"Leave it for later, she said as she walked through the door connecting their garage to the house. "Your burrito and rice are going to get cold," she said. Selecting hunger over being OCD about immediately unpacking the car, Darian grabbed a beer from the refrigerator in the garage and joined his family at the dinner table.

The Reillys ate their dinner and reminisced about the weeklong fun they had in Myrtle Beach. By the time they finished eating and unloaded the car it was nearly 11 pm. The next day was Sunday which allowed everyone to have a day of reality checks. Lisa remarked how she was going to toss the rest of the carrot cake her mom had made for them prior to leaving on vacation which had been left on the counter and crumbling.

Darian was already checking back into DigiNet with the thought that possibly his financial world may be crumbling as well.

June 22

As his iPhone alarm woke from a deep sleep, Darian slowly came to the fast realization that this was the worst day of the year:

The first day back to work after a long vacation.

Trying to muster enough strength to make it to the bathroom then down to the kitchen to let Neely out, an inward sense of doom and despair began to sink in. By now it was nearing the end of June and several bills along with the mortgage were coming due. If they were late on that, not only would their credit be tarnished but they risk losing their house as well. He realized he had to do something quickly, but he was running out of answers.

The small contracts he was used to getting at DigiNet were coming in fewer and far between, in part because of the summer but also because Media Trex was exploiting the favor of having TRW as their client. Other companies also seem to want to stand in line to do business with Media Trex since they had landed the huge international company. Even the

Westlake Porter Library deal fell through. When Gerry had asked his neighbor about the status of updating their IT system, he was told that because the levy didn't pass the previous May, all updates would be postponed indefinitely. Sensing that his friend might need to lighten the company's financial load, Gerry offered what he thought was a temporary solution.

"It would only be for a short time, until some of these contracts come in," he said to Darian. "I can get by...."

"Not a chance," Darian snapped back. "We've been through some tough times before. We'll stay afloat. Besides, I need you here to see the rest of these existing projects through to the finish line. It'll be ok, I promise."

Darian had always been a rational individual. Growing up, his family never had much money but always seemed to pull it off when they needed to. His father was an engineer on the old B&O railroad up in Michigan. Being taught to be self-sufficient from an early age made Darian capable of making adult decisions. At the age of 13 he got a job delivering newspapers to the local neighborhood. Although it wasn't much pay, it did provide him with a little spending money and taught him how to save and be disciplined. And during the cold Michigan winters, it took every bit of discipline for him to stick to his plan and do his job. Four straight years of getting up at 4am to deliver newspapers will do that to a youngster.

But every man has his breaking point. Darian did a quick analysis of DigiNet's financial situation. Lori went over the books with him along with their usual 30-60-90-day plan. The company's cash reserves were almost depleted, and their business lines of credit had been tapped out. Knowing the company was teetering on the brink of financial disaster, Lori and Darian just stared at each other, each one hoping the other would come up with something to solve this problem.

And on the home front, the Reillys were not doing too much better. Vacations have a way of drawing those extra expenses out of one's pocketbook. Darian was more and more receiving calls from creditors and bill collectors wanting to know when they would be paid. After a while he simply gave them a stock answer which was 'soon'. With their savings almost depleted and virtually no cash coming in, he was desperate to find some means to generate cash. *And he still hadn't told Lisa yet.* Since he paid all the bills it was much easier for him to keep this from her, as long as they had cash to pay for things. The one thing which gave him peace of mind was that he had a $5 million life insurance policy on himself, in the event something should happen to him. He took it out when Taylor was born and because he was still young enough, the policy with that amount was certainly affordable. Thus, Lisa and the kids would be fine. But he needed cash now. If he only had a way to tap into that. But time was running out…

June 23

For the past day or so Darian seemed to gravitate toward life insurance. He knew he had enough to protect Lisa and the kids, so it was pointless to consider purchasing a larger sum. Especially when finances were so tight. Trying to contact and recruit potential clients to the company, he stayed later than usual that night. A conference call with North Olmsted High School was scheduled for 7pm but got pushed back to nine. The city had passed a tax levy and was preparing to overhaul both the senior and junior high school buildings. The good news was the school district was cash ready and prepared to make a decision quickly. The bad news was they would not be able to tender any advances until late fall or even early January. If DigiNet were able to win the contract, Darian figured he could possibly arrange for a credit advance from Society Bank just to see them through the rough waters.

Darian got absorbed in the nuances of how to win over the NOHS contract. Gerry was going to come by the office to get on the call and told Darian he would be there by 8. Glancing at the time, Darian noticed it was 8:38. He and Gerry always got together for a pre-conference call strategy session and he still had not heard from him.

A minute later, he got a text from Nancy, Gerry's wife:

Gerry in a bad car accident. At Fairview ER now.

A blast of heat shot through him as he read the message. His first concern was for his friend and colleague. Was it serious? Was he going to be alright? He sent a quick reply:

Is he OK??? Do I need to come over??

A few minutes later Nancy texted back:

Broken arm. Not his fault. Lots of pain but will be ok. Your conference call???

That's the kind of friends Gerry and Nancy were. Despite their dire situation, Gerry knew how stressful the situation was at DigiNet and his concern was for Darian and missing the conference call. Despite the desperate need to have Gerry and his expertise on the call, Darian's chief concern was for his friend:

No worries. Take care of him and yourself. Tell him not to worry. I got this. Talk later.

Darian knew he could handle the conference call with North Olmsted by himself, but Gerry was so much better at explaining the details of how their IT systems worked and how to relate to the customer. He had that old farm boy approach that Darian lacked, and it always seemed to keep prospective customers at ease. Besides when Gerry was discussing the issues with the customer Darian would be watching and studying them to get a clue on how they were perceiving DigiNet.

Promptly at 9:01 Darian's cell phone rang. It was Mike Thompson who was the assistant principal at North Olmsted High School.

"Hello, is this DigiNet?" came Mike's inquiring voice.

"Yes, I'm here," replied Darian.

"This is Mike Thompson and I also have Sharon Moran with me here," he said. Sharon is our computer and internet guru and has forgotten way more about this than I'll ever know," he quipped.

"Great to speak to both of you, Darian said.

After explaining the situation with Gerry and receiving sympathetic comments from both Mike and Sharon, Darian pressed on with his pitch of how DigiNet can make NOHS better, stronger and faster.

The meeting took well over an hour, but Sharon continued to pepper Darian with questions. Finally, both Mike and Sharon agreed that DigiNet could definitely solve their problems and they were anxious to move forward as quickly as possible.

"We have funding approval on this project but need to have the city auditor sign off on this prior to going forward," Mike stated. "We both like what we've heard. We think your company can get us on the right track. But there is one major stumbling block which may prevent us from doing any business" he said. Darian's heart began to sink. Was it Media Trex? Did he hear about TRW? Or Cleveland Health Alliance? Can he just catch a break, just once he thought to himself??? "Can I be totally honest, Darian," Mike said.

Of course," came the stammered reply.

"You see you're in Bay Village and we're in North Olmsted. Our high school football teams have been at war since the 1960s. You've been our worst enemy in the Southwest Conference for years," as his voice trailed off.

Darian didn't know whether to laugh or cry. After what appeared to be a rather long, awkward silence, Sharon jumped in.

"He's kidding Darian. I hope you won't hold Mike's comments against us,"

Darian breathed a sigh of relief.

"Forgive me, he said. I was just reaching for some oxygen," he joked.

The three of them got a nice laugh out of it and Mike assured Darian he would be hearing from them shortly. After he hung up, Darian sat back in his office chair, reclined a bit and thought about the whole conference call. Realizing that some levity was projected on their end, that gave him a little injection of optimism about getting this deal which meant an infusion of much needed cash and getting his corporate and personal financial affairs back on track.

Lisa had taken the kids to her parents' house in Conneaut an hour away and were staying the night, so Darian was in no hurry to get home to an empty house with leftovers. He stopped at Herb's Tavern on the way home to have one of those famous Herburgers which he and Lisa always loved. Especially with a pitcher of beer to wash it down. By the time he arrived it was almost 10:30 but the kitchen was still open, even though most of the locals had gone home. He sat at the bar, which was empty, save for one other patron and ordered a Herburger, fries and a Bud Light.

"Five million dollars and I can't even touch it", exclaimed Darian to the older gentleman bartender as he finished his third beer.

"What are you talking about", the bartender replied.

"Nothing, oh it's nothing" said Darian staring right through him. Isn't it funny how an insurance company will pay your family millions of dollars once you kick the bucket, and it costs you peanuts, but you never get to see a dime of it?" he said. "If I could even cash in 5% of it my problems would be solved.

"That's why it's so cheap", replied the bartender. You're worth more dead than alive."

"I know, I know, came Darian's sharp retort. "I can't shoot myself or jump off a bridge or blow my car up. Those geniuses who wrote my life insurance policy put in a suicide clause which prevents any payment to my wife" Darian snapped.

"That's true in just about all life insurance policies" the bartender interrupted. "It's sorta like going to the dentist. When you get dental

101

coverage, you have a waiting period to get any major work done. This prevents people from buying dental insurance, getting a crown or a root canal and then submitting it for a huge claim.

"You sound just like my insurance agent," Darian quipped.

"Used to be one, once upon a time", said the bartender. "Sold life, health, auto, boat, you name it, I sold it."

Not wanting to get roped into a long biographical sketch of some bartender he hardly knew, Darian half smiled and got up to use the restroom. Thinking maybe a break in the conversation would give the bartender an opportunity to carry on with someone else, he took a few extra minutes before he returned to finish his beer. But it seemed this bartender was relentless and was not going to let Darian get away without his advice. Just then the man said something which hit Darian like a thunderbolt:

"What you need is a hit man"

Darian stood there, holding his beer just staring in silence at the man who may have possibly given him a way out. "Just make arrangements for someone to bump you off and your wife and kids live like kings for the rest of their lives."

"But how does one…."

"It has to look accidental, he interrupted. "Believe me I know what I'm talking about. I spent 36 years in this business and could detect fraud from a mile away." Darian sat back on his stool and gave the man a smirk as if to say 'that's the craziest thing I ever heard'. Without waiting for a response, the bartender, walking away shook his head and said, "you would be amazed what I have seen over the years."

"Have a good night," Darian said to the bartender as he headed for the door. "That is a stupid idea" he said to himself. Besides, where on earth would he ever find such a ruthless person willing to carry out such a scheme?

Although he lived just a few miles away, Darian decided to take an Uber home since he had more than his share of Budweiser in him. On a lark he proposed the hit man idea to his driver.

"This guy sitting near me at the bar was having an interesting conversation with the bartender and I couldn't help but overhear, Darian said to the driver. Is it true? Do people really partake in these kinds of activities?" he asked.

"Of course, you can," said the driver. "Just remember buddy, he continued, most people will do anything for the right price."

Darian stared out at the tree lined streets along Lake Rd as he crossed the border from Rocky River into Bay Village. Two different people from two different worlds gave him a similar idea. Ridiculous. There is no way. Be sensible. And besides, where on earth would he find someone to carry this out. The closer he got to home the more preposterous the idea became.

As he arrived home just in time to avoid an oncoming thunderstorm, he quickly let Neely out and grabbed her leash in anticipation of a quick walk. Living that close to Lake Erie, storms come off the lake rather quickly and Darian did not need the smell of a wet dog to cap off his night. Wandering down Inglewood Drive he couldn't help but keep his thoughts on what the bartender and the driver both said. He couldn't even fathom contacting a stranger about such a ridiculous scheme, much less carrying out a plan of execution.

"Come on girl, let's go home and get a treat," Darian shouted out to his Irish Setter. Immediately Neely turned and retreated with her master almost dragging him along. Good thing too because as soon as he opened the garage door, the heavens opened up with a vengeance. Quickly closing the garage door to keep out the rain he noticed an incredible light show courtesy of mother nature, out over the lake. Not wanting to miss out on this incredible sight, Darian kept all the lights in the house turned off and watched from their screened in patio. Flipping open his laptop to catch a little news, he wanted to see how much of a first place lead the Indians had.

Tribe up 7-2 in the eighth. Good. Need to win the division and get home field advantage, he reasoned.

Those Cleveland Indians had become a favorite of Darian's since he and Lisa arrived in Northeastern Ohio. Indeed, one of the couple's earliest dates was at a Cleveland Indians baseball game. A bit of a history buff, Darian had done some checking on his adopted team and discovered that they had not won a World Series since 1948! Sprinkled in between that World Series win and today there were a few oddball stories which happened along the way such as the relief pitcher being driven to the mound in a convertible in the 60s to ten cent beer night where the Tribe had to forfeit due to the unruly drunken fans in the 70s to "Large" Len Barker's perfect game in the 80s. It wasn't until the mid-1990s that the club started to become competitive, having reached the fall classic in both 1995 and 1997, losing the latter in a heartbreaking game 7 after leading at home in the ninth. Thus, his heart went out to this team, its fans and this city which he and Lisa had already decided to call home.

Since the Cavs started the party with an NBA Championship, maybe the Tribe can keep the ball rolling. Definitely an Indian summer he thought to himself....

June 24

A very unfamiliar light was shining through the bedroom curtains. Noticing the sun was already shining and the birds were chirping, Darian was a little confused. Was it Saturday? Where were Lisa and the kids? Did he really have that much to drink last night? What a second, he exclaimed to no one. Looking at his iPhone it was 9:22 am and it was Thursday. As he looked around, he noticed the digital clock was dark and none of the lights were working. His first thought was there must have been a power outage in the neighborhood due to last night's thunderstorm. As he walked outside to check he noticed his neighbor, Glenn Fuller operating his automatic garage door. Very strange he thought to himself. He also noticed the exterior house lights turned on at the Bailey's, just a few doors down.

Joel was afraid of the dark as a kid and insisted on keeping at least the porch light on throughout the night. As he walked back toward the garage, Darian saw what appeared to be a note attached to their mailbox. Still a little fuzzy from the sound sleep due to the late-night libations, he strolled over to the mailbox. Thinking it was some tree cutter or landscape business looking for some customers he casually checked inside the box where it was too soon for today's mail to be retrieved. He then read the attached note in utter disbelief.

A disconnection notice by First Energy Corporation!

Due to the cash crunch, he was experiencing at work and at home he had let a few of the non-credit card bills slide. In the back of his mind, he thought he had more time and was hoping the electric company would be just a little more lenient with him. Since he had not paid the bill, the power to the Reilley's home had been cut off. He raced inside and called First Energy immediately. Fortunately, since it was daylight, and no one was outside at this mid-morning hour, nobody noticed, or the word may have gotten out. He took what little he had on his debit card and restored the power within an hour.

Darian had hit an all-time low. Here he was, an educated man, who had always been prudent and careful with his money, owned his own company and now he was desperate. Thoughts of how fortunate he was would be quickly countered by bouts of depression which quickly continued to enter his mind.

Luckily, Lisa and the kids were not at home. Coming to his senses, he quickly got cleaned up, dressed, restored all the clocks in the house and grabbed an Uber to go pick up his car at Herbs. Instead of driving to the office he took a detour through the Metropark near the Huntington Playhouse where he and Lisa would attend during the season. But no more. He barely had enough cash to put gas in the car or groceries in the refrigerator.

"....most people will do anything for the right price."

Those words continued to haunt him. Here he was. A successful businessman and was brought to the brink of financial disaster. He barely was able to keep the lights on. He would have to start laying people off from work. Soon their friends and neighbors would be made aware of their situation. His club membership was going to be cancelled. Credit card companies were calling day and night. They might lose their home. His car was going to be repossessed....

"…..most people will do anything for the right price."

He pulled out his phone and looked at the photos of Lisa and the kids. How beautiful she was on their wedding day. How fortunate he was to have her as the mother of his children. What a beautiful home she had made for him. What a great life the two of them had carved out together. And Josh and Taylor being born and growing up. How fortunate he was to have two healthy, bright young children to come home to every day. He took a long look at photos of their backyard, their home, their neighborhood and their life. He went over their recent vacation pictures of their trip to Myrtle Beach, their walks along the beach at Huntington and their summer bike rides….

"…..most people will do anything for the right price."

Enough….

June 25

    Lisa texted that she and the kids were going to stay for the weekend, but he was welcome to join them at her parents' place in Conneaut. Her dad was struggling with his new computer and Lisa offered to help him retrieve some emails he had deleted. They were going to make a trip to Erie, Pennsylvania about forty-five minutes from Conneaut to the Chocolate Factory which her parents had wanted to do with Josh and Taylor for some time. They had also promised the kids a day trip to the Erie Zoo when they had visited last Easter and thought this would be a good time to go.

Lisa's dad had grown up in nearby Harborcreek and loved showing his grandkids around. His own father had an old sailboat which allowed easy access to the lake and the harbor. Although the winters were difficult to withstand, just like neighboring Cleveland, the summers were most enjoyable, but with a smaller window on the calendar. His favorite spot was on Presque Isle near the harbor area, right as the sun was setting. Coincidentally, the Chocolate Factory was within walking distance of the harbor!

Realizing that he had a few extra days to get some work done and try to bring in some much-needed revenue, Darian replied back that he will try to make it but some things at work needed his attention and he will be back in touch. Lisa, as always told him to keep checking his email.

Darian did not go into the office that day. Instead, he sent a text to Lori saying he was under the weather and would be working from home. She texted back saying that's ok and hope he feels better. Darian sent a quick reply back asking if anyone had heard from North Olmsted High School. Nothing yet, came the reply.

Knowing things were a bit slow due to the summer vacation months, he initially out of curiosity, looked into life insurance scams, how they are orchestrated and how people get caught. He knew there was no possible way for him to pull this off unless he had a third party he could trust. Not wanting to leave any cyber tracings behind, he left the house and drove to the North Olmsted Library to log onto their internet. He wanted to stay as far away from Bay Village as possible while doing his research.

Digging deeper, Darian investigated a possible individual who could do the job. He was careful to erase his history and clear search history off his browsers, even though it was a computer in a public library. He was not going to leave anything to chance.

Suddenly, he noticed something off the web which seemed to jump right off the screen:

"Having financial issues? I can take care of all your troubles for a fee. Clean and easy. Text to 216-555-3212.

Darian thought for sure it was either a scam, a trap or insurance investigators attempting to catch the bad guys. He ignored the odd invitation and pressed on. But the more he perused the web, the more his curiosity got the best of him. Finally, he sent a reply to the stranger with a simple message stating he was in need of their help.

Within 30 seconds a response came:

Meet at the Perkins on Center Ridge Rd in 30 minutes. Wear a baseball cap. Sonny.

Darian quickly glanced over his shoulder to see if anyone in the library was able to see his screen. Not being used to going to a library, he quickly caught himself and realized there was no one nearby. The new North Olmsted Branch Library was part of the Cuyahoga County System and was not even a year old. Instead of the old library which had recently been torn down and had only a handful of computers on the main table, the new library had numerous private cubicles, each equipped with its own computer to insure complete privacy.

Darian closed the browser and erased the history, something Lisa had shown him how to do. Taking it a step further, he shut down the whole computer and even unplugged it from the wall! He turned off the light and closed the door to the four foot by four-foot cubicle and cautiously walked out the door. Still convinced that someone may be able to know where he had been browsing, he jumped into the Audi and sped away. Stopping at home to pick up his Cleveland Cavaliers 2016 NBA Championship cap, he drove over to the Westlake Perkins on Center Ridge Road.

It was time to meet "Sonny".

The sunshine in the morning had given way to clouds and finally rain which pelted Lorain Rd. on the drive from the library to the Perkins restaurant in nearby Westlake. Darian felt like he was in a trance, unable to control his actions and yet still able to comprehend the magnitude of what he was about to consider. Just as the light turned green, he started to accelerate when suddenly he hit the brakes. A car had run the red light at the intersection of Dover and Center Ridge Rd. The rain had made the roads slick and the driver had nearly T-boned the Audi. A few seconds earlier, Darian thought, and his problems would have been solved.

As he approached the Perkins restaurant his heart started to race. He wasn't sure of what to expect or even if he was stepping into a world of danger to which he might not ever escape. Darian sat in his car waiting for the rain to stop, halfway convincing himself to go inside while the other half told him to get out of there as fast as he can.

The rain finally ceased. Still not able to fully believe what he was doing, he realized that it was go time. It was now or never. He knew that if he didn't do this now it would never happen. He opened his car door, locked it behind him and walked into the restaurant. Not particularly busy for this time of the afternoon. The lunchtime crowd had gone, and it was too soon for dinner. An elderly couple sat near the booth near the front door. Surveying the room, Darian caught sight of a distinguished looking gentleman sipping from a coffee cup near the back of the restaurant. Without making eye contact, Darian walked slowly toward the man's booth where he met his gaze for the first time.

"Sonny?", asked Darian in a feeble tone.

"Who's asking", replied the man.

"Clean and easy?" asked Darian.

"What can I do for you?" came the man's reply.

"I need your help, said Darian.

Before he could say anything further, the stranger stood up and gave Darian a hug as if he had known him for years. Then told him to have a seat. As Darian was sitting across from him the stranger held his index finger to his lips and showed him a text on his 'Notes' section of his phone. It read

"Empty your pockets on the table."

Darian sat nervously across from the stranger. Not sure what exactly was transpiring, after a long and awkward silence, the stranger finally spoke.

"Relax. I just needed to know you weren't wearing a wire or anything," he blurted out.

Darian, still anxious about this whole scenario, began to talk. He went on to explain how his financial situation had plummeted to the point where he had virtually no money, debts were piling up and he was desperate. Sonny listened intently for several minutes while Darian went into great detail on his $5 million life insurance policy and what needed to happen in order to remedy the situation. Finally, it was Sonny's turn to talk.

"Here's how it works, he said. I get a $2,000 non-returnable fee. You pay me now." Sonny continued. "Not to worry. It will look like an accident. I deal with your kind all the time. And you'll never know when it's coming, which is probably a good thing for you man," he said. "You have a thirty day, well let's just call it a grace period" he said.

"Grace period, what grace period? Darian asked.

"Because Sonny shot back. You rich guys always go crazy when you lose a little money. Next thing you know you want to blow your brains out or jump off a bridge and end it all. This gives you a cooling off period. In case you have a change of heart, then the deal's off. But once the thirty days is up, there's no turning back. I've already been paid so it makes no difference to me, got it? said Sonny.

"I got it," replied Darian, "but in the unlikely event I want to call this off, how do I reach you?

Without a word, Sonny reached into his coat pocket and handed him a flip phone, something he had not seen in years.

"Call the number on the back. That's how you'll reach me. You got thirty days," he repeated. If I don't hear from you by then, well you can assume your ass is mine and your next of kin will live happily ever after. "And don't lose the phone," he said with finality in his tone.

Darian, not knowing what to expect, had stopped by his commercial bank on the way to Perkins to withdraw $3,000 off his business credit line. He peeled off twenty $100 crisp new bills and passed it along the table to the man who now would take control of his life. With that, Sonny stood up, gave half smile to Darian and gave him one final warning:

"Nobody ever breaks the contract…….. Nobody."

And with that the man was gone. The man's parting words echoed in Darian's head.

June 27

Lisa and the kids pulled into the driveway close to 5 pm on Sunday just as Darian was finishing up mowing the lawn. It was a fun-filled weekend for Josh and Taylor as they always enjoyed Lisa's parents, but she was anxious to get home to her husband and get things in order after being away for a few days. Darian greeted her with a big hug and a kiss and playfully chased the kids around the yard. Everyone grabbed something out of the Suburban to bring into the house. Even Neely went crazy with Josh and Taylor since she hadn't seen them in days. The kids gathered their dirty clothes and brought them into the laundry room to form a makeshift pile, earmarked for Lisa to attack. A bit exhausted from the hour-long drive from Conneaut, she elected to table all domestic duties until tomorrow. The family decided to order pizza from Frankie's since it was quick and convenient.

Josh and Taylor were anxious to tell Darian about their adventures at the Chocolate Factory, Presque Isle and the Erie Zoo.

"We watched a baby giraffe being born", cried Taylor.

"Yeah, dad it was really cool", added Josh. "And when Taylor asked where babies come from, Pappy said I should ask you," remarked the nine-year-old.

After a brief moment of awkward silence, Darian used a simple diversion tactic to avoid answering Josh's question.

"Did Grammy and Pappy take you to the Chocolate Factory?" he asked as he and Lisa breathed a collective sigh of relief.

"Oh yes they did", Lisa interrupted with a big smile. "Go ahead guys. Show daddy." Taylor dashed away from the table and reappeared moments later with a small white box tied in a golden bow.

"Here daddy, we got this for you" the youngster exclaimed.

Darian took time out from his pizza to open the small box. Inside he couldn't help but give a half smile at what he saw. Piled neatly on top of each other were numerous different samples of chocolate fudge which they had brought home for him. There appeared to be one or two pieces missing.

"Well, said Josh slowly. When Grammy saw Pappy sneaking a piece of fudge, she grabbed the box right out of his hands."

"Yeah," said Taylor with a huge laugh. "You sure are one lucky daddy."

Darian gave his six-year-old one of his half smiles and said nothing.

Throughout the evening Lisa noticed that Darian seemed a bit quiet during dinner, electing to just drink water instead of his customary beer.

"The yard looks great" she commented as the dove into the pizza. "Looks like you really got a lot accomplished while we were away", she added.

"Yes, he said, choosing his words carefully. "I took care of some problem areas and got a lot of things cleaned up", he replied cryptically.

"No beer with your pizza, honey?" she inquired.

Darian knew the next day, Monday would be a challenge and he could not afford to let on to Lisa about their financial woes, much less the secret arrangement he had made. After all, he knew far too well that too much alcohol was the truth serum.

"No. I had a few last night and besides, I have an early day tomorrow and the last thing I need is another headache."

June 28

That last week of June came and turned into a beautiful first week of July with an Independence Day holiday upcoming. Friends and neighbors all seemed to be in a festive mood. The weather in Northeastern Ohio was great. The Flats in downtown Cleveland were buzzing. The Lake Erie Islands, particularly Put-In-Bay (the Reilly's favorite), were jam packed with boaters, partyers and assorted out of town guests. The first place Cleveland Indians were on a roll, having just swept a four-game series from those hated New York Yankees. Darian and Lisa had several dates planned with friends at Blossom Music Center down in Bath, Ohio throughout the summer, including the Cleveland Orchestra, a favorite of Lisa. Pre-season NFL Football was just around the corner and the town was hoping the Browns would return to their winning ways this year. It was a great time to be a young man with a beautiful wife and kids and a home in the suburbs to boot. Or at least it seemed that way....

July 10

Darian tried to stay focused on righting the ship, but the stress was taking its toll. He stayed at the office later and later. He had become a disciple of the calendar, carefully calculating how many days stood between now and July 25 when his thirty day "grace period" would expire. At times he would have difficulty comprehending the magnitude of what he had agreed upon. Other times it would seem like it was all a bad dream and wasn't real. At times like these many thoughts swirled around in his mind. Should he borrow money from friends or relatives? Could he call the police? Or his lawyer? Should he tell Lisa? Could he find a way to cure his financial ills in time to call off his fateful unknown date in the future with this unknown hitman? Another glance at the calendar. Fourteen days left before he would be looking over his shoulder for the rest of his life. However long or short that may be….

July 23

By now Darian had nearly reached the breaking point. By some miracle he was able keep everything concealed from Lisa while at the same time, put up a masquerade around her and the kids. He told Jack Flynn he was going easy on racquetball for the summer because his knee was acting up. This kept Darian away from River Oaks and from letting Jack Flynn know the truth about their financial woes. What little lines of credit, both business and personal Darian had access to, were dwindling it seemed by the day. He wanted less and less to go out and spend money on dinner and entertainment with friends and family. Negotiations with utility companies and creditors were becoming more common. Car payments were delayed. Phone calls from collection departments to his cell were an everyday occurrence. When the credit cards declined, he simply told Lisa the bank was being extra cautious due to the recent fraudulent activity or the payments had crossed in the mail. Lisa was no dummy, he reasoned. It was only a matter of time before she would figure things out. And now time was no longer on Darian's side....

July 24

"I have to take care of some things at the office," Darian said to Lisa as he raced out the door. "Won't be long," he shouted as he jumped into the Audi. Lisa, already late for her Saturday Yoga class waved at Darian as he pulled away.

This was Saturday. A day to get the yard work done, play with the kids and have a date night with the wife. Although just a few minutes before 9 am, the sun shone brightly, and the temperature was already a warm 78 degrees. Very few boaters on the lake so far, although Lake Erie was as smooth as glass. A few joggers making their way along Lake Road. Huntington Park was starting to get busy with people headed to the beach. A perfect morning leading into a perfect day.

Or so one thought....

Darian's thoughts were racing. He knew he had lost the fight, but he took some solace in the fact that in the end, Lisa and the kids would be financially okay. But there were other things he had never stopped to consider and now he was a mess.

Who would be there to walk Taylor down the aisle?

Or teach Josh about the birds and the bees?

Who would take Neely on her walks to Huntington Park?

Who will be there to grow old with Lisa?

Or their neighborhood cookouts?

Or their beautiful life?

Darian had always looked at the business side of this arrangement. Now it had hit him that the human side of it has consequences as well. A myriad of emotions ran through his mind as he made his way to the office. By this time tears were streaming down his face and he was powerless to stop them. He didn't even look at the calendar these past few days as he knew he was unable to put a stop to what he had put in place.

As he turned off Crocker Bassett Rd and pulled into his office parking lot, empty on a Saturday, he sat there in his Audi in all his despair. Given that it was such a beautiful Saturday morning, Darian elected to drive with the windows down and the top open. He had hoped the gentle July morning breezes would calm him a bit but to no avail.

As he sat motionless in the parking lot and wondering how it all came to this, he couldn't help but hear a strange buzzing coming from inside the car. As he looked around, he noticed his phone had fallen between the console and the passenger seat. This buzzing sound was coming from his phone. Another bill collector, he figured. As he reached the device, he noticed it wasn't a call but a text. Glancing at the home screen he saw several text messages from Gerry.

"Call me asap" came the same message five times in a row.

Thinking Gerry was in some sort of trouble or needed help at his farmhouse, he hit Gerry's number on speed dial.

"Have you heard? Gerry yelled into the phone.

"Heard what?" replied Darian.

"Dude you are not going to believe this. We have just been awarded the Midwest Regional Homeland Security contract." Gerry shouted.   It's an $8.5 million dollar contract and it was awarded to DigiNet!"

Darian gasped. For a second, he could not talk.

"Gerry," he said calmly, are you telling me what I think you're telling me?"

"Abso-Flockin-Lutely" Gerry shouted again. "Didn't you see the email? It was sent to you and I was copied on it. Where the hell are you?"

Darian had to catch his breath.

"As a matter of fact, I'm at the office right now. Call you back."

Darian tried to stay calm as he fumbled with his keys to get out of the car and into the office. As he waited for his computer and the server to boot up, it seemed like an eternity. Could this be? Are we ok? No more sleepless nights? He can finally relax and enjoy life again?

Sure enough, time stamped Friday July 23 4:09 pm the subject line stated

Government Contract Awarded

As Darian read through the email it went on to state the words that he had been working for his entire life:

The United States Dept of Homeland Security is pleased to award the Midwest Contract for Inland Security to DigiNet Corporation of Cleveland, Ohio.

Darian sat back in his chair. He looked at the clock. It was 9:33 am. He read the rest of the email along with the attachments depicting all the details of the deal. DigiNet would receive a $2,000,000 advance for initial expenses with the balance paid to them on or before September 30, the last day of the government's fiscal year.

He could hardly believe it. His company was saved. His family was going to be ok. Everything he had ever worked for was now going to pay off handsomely. He had to get to work on this immediately. A thousand details had to be worked out. Hire more employees to handle the increased workload. Pay the existing staff overtime to meet deadlines. Lori will need a raise to help oversee this. More time spent at the office. He reached for his phone to call Lisa to tell her the good news. He noticed the calendar on his phone had the number "24" on it.

Darian's exuberance had immediately turned to panic. He opened his calendar app on his phone and began to count the days from the day he made the deal with Sonny, June 25, until today. He repeated the task several times. He was given a 30 day "grace period" from Sonny in case he wanted to back out. Those words from the unscrupulous hitman came back to him plain as day:

"You rich guys always go crazy when you lose a little money. Next thing you know you want to blow your brains out or jump off a bridge and end it all. This gives you a cooling off period. But once the thirty days is up, there's no turning back. Nobody ever breaks the contract……Nobody."

"Let's see, Darian thought to himself. "From June 25 until today is only 29 days. I need to call this nut immediately to let him know the deal is off." Frantically, he raced out of his office to his car, jumped in and headed for home. Thinking that his fate had indeed been sealed a few days back, Darian had left the cell phone Sonny had given him in his briefcase which was in his office at home. Random thoughts again raced through his head, this time between euphoria from being awarded the government contract and outright fear of being bumped off at the next turn. He had time, he reasoned.

According to Darian's count he had one more day to reach Sonny and tell him the deal was off. As he pulled into the neighborhood, he waved to several of the neighbors who were out getting a jump on their Saturday yard work. Not bothering to pull into his garage, he raced into the house where Josh and Taylor were just finishing their breakfast.

"Hi daddy," shouted Taylor. Are we going to the bookstore today? You promised, Daddy.

"Of course, we are sweetie," Darian responded. "But first I have to take care of something very important".

Reaching his office in the lower level, he opened his briefcase and searched for the phone.

Nothing.

He dumped the contents out onto the floor.

Nothing.

He checked his desk and hutch drawers. No sign of the henchman's cell phone.

"What the hell did I do with that phone?" Darian shouted to himself.

Out of his office and out to his car he ran. Did he leave it in the car? Lisa's car? The office? He had been under an enormous amount of stress and pressure the last few days that he never thought he would be contacting Sonny to tell him the deal was off. He raced back to the office and turned the place inside out.

Nothing.

Lisa arrived home shortly thereafter, armed with enough groceries to feed the entire Ohio National Guard. Darian, still frantically searching for the phone, stopped to help her load them into the house.

"Are you ok," said Lisa as she noticed her husband sweating and behaving oddly.

"I'm fine. I'm just looking for something that I absolutely must find." he replied.

"Well, what is it," she inquired.

"It's a phone. A cell phone. I am missing a cell phone, alright?" he snapped.

"Ok Ok, she shot back. Your phone is over there by the toaster."

"Not my regular phone, another phone I was given…." his voice trailed off.

"What do you mean you were given, she asked. Did someone give you a phone? Who would give you a phone?"

"Never mind, Darian shot back. I'll take care of this myself."

"Well while you're out there saving lives can you at least go pick up the dry cleaning?" she barked at him. "They close in less than an hour and your shirts and your charcoal suit are ready."

Without saying a word, Darian jumped into his car and headed over to Bee Clean Dry Cleaners on Dover Rd. Arriving there just prior to closing, he was handed the stack of shirts and his charcoal suit by a young man working behind the counter. Not caring whether or not his newly dry cleaned and pressed clothes were hung up nice and neat or in a wrinkled pile, he threw them into the trunk of the Audi and jumped into the driver's seat getting ready to race off.

Suddenly, the young man who had handed him the dry cleaning stopped him.

"What is it," shouted Darian.

"I'm sorry Mr. Reilly but is this yours?" the young man sheepishly asked.

Glancing up, Darian saw the boy holding something in his hand.

The missing cell phone.

"It was in one of the pockets of your suit and must have fallen out", he explained.

"My God," said Darian. "Yes, it is mine. I can't tell you what this means to me. Thank you." Darian said as he flipped the young man a five-dollar bill.

He then felt a surge of relief come over him that he hadn't felt in months. Reaching down he went to dial the number and make the call. What he heard next sent him into a frenzy:

The number you have dialed has been disconnected or is no longer in service....

After leaving the dry cleaners and recovering the missing cell phone, Darian took the long way home after leaving the office in order to clear his head. He had not prepared himself for such an up and down turn of events and certainly had to look and act normal in front of Lisa and the kids. By now the beautiful Northern Ohio morning had given way to a typical mid-July hot summer afternoon.

"Lindsey is watching the kids tonight," Lisa said to Darian as he arrived home. Did you make it to the dry cleaners?" she asked.

"Yes, yes I made it. Oh crap, my suit. I left it in the trunk of the car" he responded.

"Daddy is going cuckoo", Taylor laughed as she watched her dad scurry back out to the car.

"He sure is, replied Lisa. Keep drying the dishes honey. I'll help daddy with the dry cleaning."

Lisa dried her hands and marched out to the driveway where she met her disheveled husband. As he tried to put the newly wrapped clothes on his finger, he felt a firm hand grasp him on his arm.

"What is it? What the hell is going on?" his perceptive wife asked. Is there something wrong?"

"No, no. I'm sorry. It's been one hell of a morning", he said with a sigh.

Hesitating for a moment, Darian then pulled out his phone and showed the email he had received from the Office of Homeland Security. Lisa, no amateur with email immediately knew this was no joke.

"Oh my God, she shouted. Is this for real? Does this mean…"

"Yes, it does, baby", he said, interrupting her.

Lisa threw her arms around her husband then kissed him repeatedly. Tears of joy ran down her face as she was overcome with an abundance of emotion. Still, after a minute of holding on to Darian, she was hardly able to speak.

"I am so proud of you and I love you so much", her voice barely louder than a whisper.

"I love you too Lisa, he responded, still holding her in the middle of their driveway. I'm sorry I've been acting like such an ass."

"It's ok, it's ok", she interrupted, still fighting off tears of joy.

"But I really need your help with something", Darian said.

"What, what is it?" his ecstatic wife asked.

"Please, honey…. help me untangle this damn dry cleaning!!!!"

Darian was equally trying to fight off the emotional high of the day's events but tempered his euphoria with the knowledge that he had one small detail he had to take care of. Given the high that he and Lisa were on at the moment, he reasoned that this Sonny character will be willing to make a deal and he will shortly be out of the picture.

July 25

Darian failed to set his alarm clock on his iPhone the night before, but he and Lisa enjoyed a lazy, Sunday morning and caught up on some much-needed sleep. Even Neely refrained from waking Darian with her customary kisses anticipating her morning weekend walk.

"I'll start breakfast, you take Neels for her walk and I'll meet you and the kids downstairs" Lisa instructed. Darian reached over and gave his wife a kiss, jumped out of bed and headed for the door. Neely raced down the stairs and waited for her master at the front door.

As he corralled the Irish setter on her leash and navigated the sun-drenched streets of Bay Village, Darian's head was spinning now. He and Lisa had enjoyed a perfect evening out the night before listening to the Cleveland Orchestra at Blossom Music center near Akron. As the evening wore on the two of them discussed the future and things they might now possibly be able to do. Lisa was always a practical, clear thinking individual, something which attracted him to her but now she seemed like she was at peace. They now could talk about dreams of travel, redecorating their home, maybe purchase a beach house and not worry as much about where Josh and Taylor would be spending their college days.

But Darian still had a mess he had to fix. He needed to get in touch with this lunatic hitman with whom he had foolishly made arrangements. He thought about discussing this with Jack Flynn who was a close friend and, also an attorney, but he was ashamed of entering into such a stupid and illegal agreement to begin with. If he could only reach Sonny and offer him a monetary sum to make him go away. This sounded reasonable but who knows, when you are dealing with a member of the underworld.

"There has to be a way to get to this guy before he gets to me," he said to Neely. She frequently was his sounding board when it came to issues he had had in the past and he really needed her to listen now!

July 26

It was now Monday morning and Darian left early for the office to try to recover from a highly emotional roller coaster weekend. He had experienced the depths of despair while sitting in his car on Saturday morning thinking his life was over, only to discover his company had then realized a financial windfall. But the euphoria was short-lived as he was unable to reach Sonny on the cell phone he had been given and now he realized it was too late. He knew he had to keep his eyes open and his head together.

"Wow, congratulations boss" shouted Lori across the room to Darian as he walked through the front door.

"Thanks, but we have a lot of work to do" came Darian's terse reply.

"*Hmmm*, Lori thought to herself. *If I had been awarded an $8 million contract, I'd be doing cartwheels.*"

Darian closed his office door and jumped into the chair. He knew he needed to address his staff on the good news but at the same time he had to deal with this Sonny situation. He could not tell anyone, not his friends, not the police and certainly not Lisa. He texted Lori to have everyone in the conference room in 30 minutes for a Midwest Homeland Security strategy session.

"I'm sorry but once a number has been deleted from a prepaid phone it goes into our database of dead phone numbers and is non traceable," came the friendly Verizon customer service representative on the other end of the phone. "People use these phones for advertising and scams and as result, certainly don't want to be traced," she offered.

Darian thanked the woman for her time and hung up. The news of the phone company's failure to track or trace someone just added to his Monday morning uneasiness.

He then met with his staff later that morning and tried his best to put on a smiley face which would be normal for someone who had just been awarded an $8.5 million government contract. He also knew he had work to do and had to move forward.

Lisa had spent her usual Monday morning tackling the laundry and household duties while Taylor and Josh were finishing their breakfast. Mondays were always grocery days in the Reilly family and today was no exception. Following a quick cleanup of the breakfast dishes, she instructed the kids to get in the car as they were headed to Giant Eagle.

Josh and Taylor were extremely helpful picking out their favorite breakfast cereal as well as dog food for Neely while Lisa concentrated on the more critical items such as what to have for dinner the entire week. With their cart filled to capacity as usual, they headed for the checkout. Remembering her husband had appeared to be a bit stressed out these last few days, Lisa decided to grab a fresh bottle of Catawba wine which she knew he loved. As she commandeered the overloaded shopping cart over to the wine section, she carefully looked over the enormous selection that Giant Eagle afforded.

Suddenly there was a huge jolt. Her cart had crashed into another cart being pushed by a rather peculiar looking man.

"I'm so sorry" Lisa apologized. I wasn't even looking where I was going."

The man stared at Lisa for a moment saying nothing, hesitated, then finally spoke saying "it's quite alright. You'll be fine."

Lisa grabbed a bottle of a Red Cabernet and hastened to the checkout aisle. The man, dressed in black, disappeared from the store. Lisa thought it was a bit odd that the man she had run into at Giant Eagle had nothing in his cart, spoke hardly at all and was suddenly gone from the store. She thought about it so much she completely forgot to get gas on the way home.

"Mom can we ride our bikes down the old railroad path?" asked Josh as they pulled out of the Giant Eagle parking lot.

"Well, we'll see" she responded making her way north on Dover Center Rd. "Remember pretty soon we will have to start practicing getting to bed earlier you guys as school is right around the corner", Lisa announced to Josh and Taylor. The collective groan by her nine- and six-year-old simply forced a slight smile on their mom's face which indicated disdain and agreement.

Crossing over I-90 and then the railroad tracks signifying the boundary from Westlake into Bay Village, Lisa took advantage of the red light at Knickerbocker Rd. to send Darian a quick text asking if he will be home on time. Her husband responded quickly with a thumb's up emoji and a red heart saying, "I love you."

"Look mommy, there's your friend from the store" exclaimed Taylor as they pulled their Suburban onto Inglewood Drive.

The smile Lisa had from reading Darian's text turned to one of mild to moderate concern as she noticed it was the same man she had run into at Giant Eagle. He was standing a block away from their home. Lisa drove the Suburban past the man and into their garage. Thinking there might be something suspicious, she casually walked out to the street to pretend to get the mail. Upon reaching the mailbox near the curb she noticed the man was no longer there. Strange coincidence, she surmised.

The familiar roar of the Audi A6 was heard shortly after 6pm that afternoon. Darian pulled up the driveway and got out to be met by his faithful companion, Neely. He greeted Lisa with a hug and a kiss then ran out back to greet the kids. All seemed well in suburban Bay Village. Lisa had dinner on the table as Darian, Taylor and Josh came marching in.

As the evening ensued, Darian filled Lisa in on the details of the government contract. Lisa could still not believe her ears.

"I'm so proud of you honey, she exclaimed. You have worked so hard for this and you deserve every bit of this. Now when can we redecorate?" she laughed half-jokingly.

Darian had been so engulfed with the Homeland Security Contract and all the details all day that he had somewhat forgotten about Sonny. Lisa brought out the bottle of the Red Cabernet to celebrate. As she poured her husband a glass she was reminded of the strange events of the day.

"Funny thing happened at Giant Eagle today, " she said. "As I was trying to locate this Red Cab, I accidentally ran my cart into the cart of another gentleman at the store.

"Well, what's so incredible about that, other than you shouldn't drink and drive a shopping cart" he quipped.

"Funny thing was, the man I bumped into had nothing in his cart, just stared at me for a moment and then told me 'you'll be alright.'"

"Maybe he just got to the store and had not decided on what to purchase yet," reasoned Darian.

"But then, Lisa continued, as we turned onto our street, I noticed him again standing about three doors down from us, in front of the Bailey's house."

"What did this guy look like?" Darian asked as he put down his glass of wine and leaned forward in his chair.

"Well, Lisa said, "he had on a black suit with no tie on, just a black T-shirt, you know, instead of a business dress shirt on."

Darian's face froze. He soon realized that the man she was describing was this hitman and may be closing in on making good on his promise.

"Did you call the police? asked Darian.

No, why should I" asked Lisa. "It just seemed strange to run into a person at a grocery store then see them later that same day on your street."

Darian was a mess. He tried to keep it together in front of Lisa, but she was too smart for that. "What is it honey, what's wrong? she asked? Something is wrong and you're not telling me."

"Nothing, nothing, he stammered. Everything is going to be fine; I promise you."

July 27

Darian was in a tailspin. He was so busy with the government contract and all the details that went with it, yet at the same time he was trying to stay alive! He was not getting much sleep. His eating habits had changed dramatically, and several their friends had noticed a change in him as well. Enough is enough, he reasoned. That night he made a decision. Realizing that Sonny was getting closer by the day he had to make a plan to get away from Lisa and kids, if for no other reason, their safety. He also had to tell Lisa somehow, someway the whole story. And none of this would be easy.

He composed an email to her instead of a handwritten note figuring this way only she would be able to read it. Didn't want to leave a letter on paper around where someone else might find it. After several failed drafts, he was finally able to compose what he thought was the best descriptive writing to her with the subject line blank.

Several times Darian thought about hitting the send button and leaving but he knew he had to wait for just the right moment. He left the email in his draft folder for the moment then checked on a few text messages before diverting his attention back to his emails. Then it hit him: While he knew he needed to distance himself from his wife and kids for their own safety, he also needed to locate this Sonny guy and try to negotiate some sort of settlement and put an end to this arrangement. Sonny was a businessman, Darian thought, and the Uber driver's remarks kept coming back to him:

"most people will do anything for the right price..."

Darian hit the delete button and moved the email to Lisa out of his outbox. And maybe get Sonny out of his life.

July 28

Josh had football tryouts from 6-8 so Darian thought tonight would present the perfect opportunity to put his plan in motion since Lisa and Taylor would be at the tryouts hanging with the other moms. He sent her a short text hoping she would buy into his subterfuge:

Had to buzz up to Detroit. New client. Back tomorrow hopefully. Love u

Upon seeing the text from her husband while chatting with the other football moms, Lisa thought this to be a bit odd as Darian never went out of town on a day's notice since it was so expensive to travel and also because his schedule had recently become so demanding. Especially with the new government contract occupying most of his time. But given the recent success which DigiNet had enjoyed, she gave him the benefit of the doubt and quickly dismissed her suspicions.

The harsh whistle of the 4th grade football coach pierced the summer evening. Practice was over. The tryouts were complete. Parents gathered around to get some preliminary instructions on what happens next in terms of playing time, schedules and practices. However, Lisa could *still* not get it out of her head that something was up with Darian. Was it a problem at work? A health issue? A financial problem? Another woman? Nothing made any sense to her. She and Taylor walked with Josh back to the car and headed for home. Upon arriving home, noticing Darian's car was not in the garage, yet his overnight bag had not been packed, she started to panic.

Something was wrong!

She prepared a quick dinner for Taylor and Josh.

"Aren't you going to eat with us, mommy?" yelled Josh from the kitchen.

"I'll be there in a minute," Lisa shouted back. She was in Darian's office rifling through drawers, looking for some kind of clue which would shed light on this. He always called her before heading out of town but today there was no phone call from him at all.

With Darian's laptop sitting on his desk, using his password 28924LJT she quickly gained access to his system. She checked his web browser history, but it had all been deleted. Not a good sign. His cache had been deleted and his emails were also gone. Checking the deleted folder, she noticed it was empty. Seemingly at a dead end, she thought about one other way: Using her email expertise, she tapped into the server and typed in the command:

Recover Deleted Items from Server

Suddenly, dozens of emails came pouring in sorted by date. Realizing that most of these were personal and not business in nature, she then sorted them by whom they were sent to. Since Darian and Lisa emailed and texted regularly, she found most of them were sent to her. Then she sorted them by subject line and painstakingly glanced through each. She then noticed one which did not have anything in the subject line. Very odd since Darian always loved leaving cute little teasers in the subject line for her. As she began to read the unusual email, thoughts of horror and disbelief ran through her head as this truth-is-stranger-than-fiction story unfolded right before her eyes as she read her husband's goodbye letter to herself:

My Darling Lisa,

We have shared so many wonderful times together and the life we have made is far beyond what I could have ever imagined I would get. But a dark cloud has been cast over me and I made a decision. While we were failing financially earlier this year, I became desperate and depressed. I made an arrangement, a contract if you will, with a man to execute me but to make it look like an accident or an unlawful act.

This arrangement was made a month ago and I was given time to back out but since we were so far in debt and I was not thinking clearly, I went forward with the arrangement. It will happen sometime in the near future I suspect and here's why. The man you ran into at the grocery store whom you also saw on our street is the man I made this arrangement with.

I wish I could go back in time and undo what I have committed to do but unfortunately that is not possible. I made several attempts to reach this man but with no success. You, Josh and Taylor will have the $5 million *from my life insurance once this is all over. That will be more than enough*

to sustain you and the kids for years to come. Please know that you cannot

show this to anyone as it may come back to haunt you legally and

financially. Also, please understand that I always had you and the kids in

mind when I entered into this arrangement.

I will always be with you.

All my love,

Darian

She slumped back in her husband's office chair, now sobbing uncontrollably. She hid her head in her hands shaking back and forth while trying to control her despair so her children wouldn't hear her but to no avail. She glanced at her phone's GPS and noticed Darian's location services were still enabled. He was parked at a Red Roof Inn in nearby Vermillion, about 40 miles west of Bay Village.

"What's wrong, mommy? Why are you crying?" asked Taylor. Josh looked at his mom with confusion in his eyes. Without saying a word, Lisa grabbed her phone and called her friend Maggie from down the street.

"For God's sake Mag get over here quick" she barked into the phone. Maggie was there inside of a minute. "I have to go out for a bit, won't take long. Can you watch Josh and Taylor for me please?" Maggie and her husband, Joel had been trying to start a family for over a year and always cherished taking care of their friend's children.

"Sure, no problem. Go" shouted Maggie as Lisa ran out the door.

By this time darkness had settled in over Northeastern Ohio and Greater Cleveland. Lisa jumped into her Suburban and headed for Ohio State Route 2. Adding to her woes was the fact that she had cursed herself for not filling up on gas earlier in the week. The quick stop at the BP off Bassett Rd seemed like an eternity. Following Darian's location, she soon found herself in a much more rural area than where they lived. She and Darian had passed this way many times on their way to East Harbor State Park, Cedar Point and the Lake Erie Islands, but she never really paid much attention.

A billboard up ahead showed multiple Red Roof locations within the next several miles. One was 4 miles ahead while the other was 17 miles ahead. The latter coincided with the location Darian was showing on the Location Services app on her phone. Lisa had to watch her speed as she realized she couldn't afford a delay by getting pulled over by an Ohio State Trooper but still realized that time was of the essence.

Darian had left the office about 5:30 and immediately headed west. Stopping at a neighborhood Shell on Lake Rd in Rocky River, he gassed up his Audi and jumped in the car. As he placed the key in the ignition, he looked in his rear-view mirror and noticed a familiar face. Sonny was parked across the street in the Cleveland Clinic parking lot. After making eye contact with him and noticing the .38 special he had tucked in his pants, Darian panicked, hit the gas and jumped onto I-90 westbound which quickly turned into Ohio State Route 2. Looking in his rear-view mirror he saw Sonny make an immediate turn and attempt to head west on the freeway in pursuit.

Darian had to think fast. And drive fast. His speeds at one point exceeded 110 miles per hour and he quickly realized he was dead if he were to get pulled over. Thinking he had a comfortable lead, he headed west out past Avon and Lorain and found a Red Roof Inn off Route 2 near Vermillion. He quickly parked his Audi in the back of the motel in a remote spot, hoping not to be seen. He checked into a room which had the highest viewpoint so he could keep watch.

Looking at his phone he saw it was almost 9pm and he had not eaten all day. Better to eat something and stay alert, he reasoned. But he couldn't risk leaving the motel. With nothing in the vicinity, he called down to the main office asking if there were takeout anywhere. The manager on duty said not in the immediate area but he could order some wings from across the street for him. Darian said that would be fine and there's a $20 tip in it for whoever brings the food up to room 409. The manager said fine, he would be there in about 20 minutes and hung up.

About a half hour later there was a knock on the door. Darian, eager to get something in his stomach, muted the flat screen TV, reached for his wallet and opened the door.

It was Sonny.

"Move away from the door, chief," came the hitman's gruff and raspy tone while he pointed his .38 at his elusive quarry. Darian, totally caught off guard, and wondering now whether he was going to live or die, stepped away and tried to reason.

"Now look, you don't understand, he pleaded. Things are different. I can pay you to walk away. Let me do this now and nobody gets hurt," he said, shaking.

"Let's go," said Sonny as he led Darian away.

Out the door and down the steps the two men walked. Spotting the Audi on the other side of the parking lot, Sonny gave the instructions.

"Get in, you drive," he commanded. Darian, trying to find a quick way out, made several attempts to reason with Sonny.

"My company just hit a financial windfall. I can pay you more than what I had previously.

"You could be a setup, or with the cops or the FBI," barked out Sonny, holding the gun on Darian as he got behind the wheel.

"There's no way," shot back Darian. I'd go to prison if this all came out. Look, I was desperate but that's over now. My company has money, and I can…..

"SHUT UP", yelled the hitman. I didn't come here to yack. Pull around here, down this dirt road." Shut the car off and place the keys on the dash…. NOW."

Sonny stepped out of the car, with the gun still pointed at his prey. Coming around to the driver's side, he kept the gun pointed at Darian's head, and started to yell louder.

"You rich guys think you own the rest of us…..you think we can be bought and sold…you think you have all the power…well who has the power now, huh?"

"Remember nobody ever breaks the contract, chief. Nobody," shouted the henchman.

Suddenly a car with no headlights came shooting down the dirt road. Sonny, still pointing the gun at his defenseless victim, glanced to his right as he saw the car approaching. Sensing a possible opportunity to escape, Darian clenched the inside door handle and whipped open the driver's door of his Audi, throwing Sonny backwards into the vulnerable path of the oncoming car. Because of the dirt road, the brakes of the car did not squeal as it approached the pair rapidly.

Smash!

That thunderous sound of when a car has struck a pedestrian now was more real than ever. Darian jumped out and saw Sonny lying on the ground motionless. Completely in shock, he glanced up at the car with its headlights now turned on, temporarily blinding him. He heard the slamming of a car door and the sound of rushing footsteps of an unknown person approaching him.

Lisa!

Both husband and wife stared down in silence at the prone body of the person who almost changed their lives forever. Falling into each other's arms, they were trying to come to grips with what had just happened. For a moment, neither one said a word.

Finally, Darian said, "let's get out of here."

The young couple each jumped into their respective cars and sped away. Sonny lay there in a deserted field, off a deserted road, off a rural highway.

Stunned silence was the melody that played on repeat the rest of the night. Nothing was said the night it happened. Darian and Lisa had arrived home that night shortly before 11 pm and long after Maggie had put Josh and Taylor to bed. Darian followed his wife into the house but said nothing and made no eye contact as he passed Maggie in the kitchen and went up to their bedroom.

"Are you alright? Is everything ok?" Maggie asked.

"Yes, yes, thank you, came Lisa's reply. Darian was in an accident and needed help and I'm sorry I just ran out like that," she cried to her friend.

"Lisa, please it's ok," Maggie replied. I'm so glad the two of you are ok."

Both mentally and emotionally exhausted from the experience, Lisa and Darian, still in shock over the entire incident, climbed into bed, laid awake in the darkness and said nothing to each other.

July 29

The next morning Darian left early for the office and tried to get back into a relatively normal state of emotions. He had to think clearly and move fast. The Homeland Security contract in the upcoming days would require his full attention. The matter of an unknown thug coming after him from around the next corner was now a thing of the past. Perhaps life could get back to normal with DigiNet, his friends and of course, Lisa.

Arriving home past dinner time, Darian joined Lisa, Josh and Taylor at the dinner table while they were just finishing up. School was starting in just a few weeks and the kids were buzzing about all the back-to-school items Lisa had purchased for them. Throughout the meal Darian and Lisa periodically exchanged long, blank stares at each other. Small talk was made between them in front of the children. Since tomorrow was the last day at Huntington Day Camp for both, Lisa had the kids in bed early for the night. Darian had just come back from a long walk with Neely. He stopped by both kids' rooms, tucked them both in and said goodnight.

"What the fuck were you thinking, Lisa cried as he closed the door to their master bedroom behind him. "I cannot even fathom anyone partaking in this kind of a scheme, let alone someone as educated as yourself," she barked. "How fucking stupid can you be?" Do you realize the danger you put us in? And you? And our children? You make a deal with some lunatic whom you don't even know, and you nearly get yourself killed? Lisa went on and on for several minutes, half crying, half yelling, conveying to her husband how frightened she was upon reading his email while at the same time feeling somewhat insulted that he would not confide in her about a situation this serious.

"I wasn't thinking," came Darian's reply. The only explanation I can give is that I wanted to make sure you and the kids were safe and provided for should anything happen to me."

"You're damn right you weren't thinking," she thundered. The fact that you came within an eyelash of being left for dead in some corn field.... good God Darian, what the hell is wrong with you?"

"I know, I know, I know," he shouted back to her. I was desperate. I was at the end of my freaking rope Lisa. Can't you understand that?" he yelled.

The verbal shots went back and forth for several more minutes. After a while, both husband and wife sat silent for a minute. Both were emotionally drained. Then Lisa appeared to calm down as her voice softened almost to a whisper.

"Darian, sweetheart. I love you. For better or for worse, remember?" she said as she knelt in front of him while he sat on the edge of the bed. "It's always been you and me. Us against the world. We have been so much a part of each for so long. We could have fixed this together," she said calmingly.

Darian nodded in agreement, his eyes now full of emotion as he realized the pain and fear he had inflicted upon his wife. The conversation continued well into the evening. Finally, resigned to the fact that their family was out of danger, they both climbed into bed, kissed and made up, enjoyed each other then fell asleep, exhausted.

July 30

Darian had gotten an early start the next morning to prepare DigiNet for the massive task of providing the US Department of Homeland Security the necessary internet security it was expecting. Arriving at the office just before 7am, he flipped on his laptop, sipped his morning coffee and sat back in his chair. The events of the previous 48 hours had really taken its toll on him emotionally, but he knew he had to focus on the task at hand and move forward. In addition, the North Olmsted High School Board had approved the contract with DigiNet and although it did bring in more revenue to the company, it was going to stretch the corporate personnel resources that much thinner.

Darian had Lori schedule a meeting with everyone in the company for 9am. She was always an early riser and usually got to the office before anyone else, except for her boss, of course. Gerry arrived shortly before 8am carrying a huge box of Dunkin Donuts and a huge smile on his face.

"Morning boss," his second in command shouted as he stopped by Darian's office. "How does it feel to be able to exhale again," he quipped.

"You have no idea," his boss replied with a sheepish half smile.

"I know, I know," Gerry responded as he walked toward the lunchroom to deposit the box of donuts.

Oh, know you don't, Darian thought to himself.

The day seemed to fly by. Since the whole staff was going to be involved in this new venture, Darian had Lori order lunch in for everyone from the Rocky River Brewing Company.

"Once the dust settles and we have a handle on this Homeland Security Contract, we can *go* to the Brewery for lunch but today everyone needs to stay focused and know what job they have to do," Darian announced.

Sparing no expense for his hard-working employees, they had their choice of cooked salmon, steak, chicken, shrimp and all the sides and salads. Years earlier, Lisa had suggested that if DigiNet ever hit it big, those hard-working employees needed to be rewarded financially. Darian couldn't agree more.

It was nearly 4pm when he and Gerry were deep in a strategy session when a text appeared on his phone.

"Dinner and beers at Herb's tonight with Maggie and Joel. Don't be late. Love you!"

Of course, Darian had forgotten. What with everything that had transpired the last two days as well as trying to get the Homeland Security contract going. He was actually planning to work well into the evening that first day but then realized what he had put his wife through such an ordeal that she deserved an evening out with her husband anyway, so he quickly texted her back:

"No way did I forget. Very busy here but can't wait to get home. Love U2"

The strategy session with Gerry ended just before 5pm. Lori wandered into Darian's office trying to cover up a huge smile on her face.

"Check this out, Boss," she said as she handed him her laptop. Numerous times in the past few months Lori had the unpleasant task of handing Darian her laptop which only meant the cash in the corporate account was dwindling.

Lori was a native Ohioan who grew up on the west side of Cleveland. She was able to work her way through Magnificat High School, working part time and became a starter on the girls' volleyball team. She was somewhat spoiled when the Blue Streaks won the State Finals her sophomore, junior and senior years and Lori was a huge part of their success, starting all three years.   After receiving scholarship offers from various universities around the area, she decided to stay closer to home because her dad had been stricken with bone cancer. Lori chose to enroll in the Monte Ahuja School of Business at Cleveland State University with a dual major in finance and economics.   When her dad passed away in the fall of her junior year, she decided to take some accelerated courses the following summer and graduated a semester ahead of her class in order to get the jump on the job market. Answering an ad for a small IT startup company which called itself DigiNet, she and Darian clicked from the very first interview. Never mind that she was tall and attractive and a former Miss Cuyahoga County runner-up. Darian just wanted someone whom he could trust to run the store while he could focus on other things. Lori also knew from her business education that sometimes these small startups can turn into large corporations which tend to reward their employees financially.

"Don't tell me, let me guess, Darian said, feigning confusion. Is it the Girl Scouts selling cookies?   No, wait, it's a fundraiser for the Magnificat Volleyball team," he joked.

"I'm really going to smack you," she said as she dangled her laptop in front of him. "You know why they call this a laptop boss, she asked. Because I'm about to dump this into your lap now sit up and pay attention," she commanded with a smile.

"Yes ma'am," Darian replied with a salute.

Darian looked at the online bank register which Lori had downloaded. Sure enough, on the deposit side of the ledger was an entry dated July 30 with the depositor listed as "United States Government. The amount was $2,000,000.

"I guess some days you're the windshield and some days you're the bug," Lori laughed as she snatched her laptop back from her boss. The young entrepreneur just smiled.

"Are you able to set up a separate insurance account with the bank for this deposit?" he asked her.

"Already took care of that, " she said. The funds will transfer after midnight into the new account which is totally insured against loss up to five million. We can transfer back into the operating account as often as we wish with no fee or penalty."

"Great job, Lori, her boss replied. As usual you think in paragraphs while I think in sentences, he added. And speaking of windshields, you better get behind yours and get the hell out of here. Go home, relax and I'll see you tomorrow." Lori grabbed her laptop, went back to her office, logged out and left. Darian shut off the lights, locked the office and headed for home. Maggie and Joel were meeting him and Lisa at Herb's at 7pm and for a change, he could relax and enjoy life again.

Darian pulled into the driveway just after 6pm. Lisa had already prepared dinner for the kids while waiting for Lindsey, their neighbor's daughter to arrive to sit for a few hours. "Hello, hello everyone," Darian said as he greeted Lisa with a big kiss. How are we doing, favorite children of mine," he asked his two youngsters.

"Dad, exclaimed Josh, guess what. I made the football team first string middle linebacker. We have our first game on Sunday, the youngster said.

"I am so proud of you buddy, " Darian replied. When do you get your uniforms?

"This Saturday. Will you go with me? I have to get fitted for gamepads and uniforms, stuff like that,"

"And Taylor is a finalist on the junior cheerleading squad," Lisa chimed in.

"That's awesome, sweetie," said Darian. Do you know any cheers yet?" he asked. You know your mom was a cheerleader in high school so I'm sure she could teach you a few things. In fact, one of her favorite cheers was this one:

Siss boom bee, kick em in the knee

Siss boom bass, kick em in the… …

"Darian!!" shouted his interjecting wife. "Guys, I think aliens have come down to earth and replaced your daddy with this weirdo," she stated. "Don't worry, I'm sure your *real* Daddy will be back soon," she said as she stared down her husband.

Josh and Taylor giggled and laughed at the exchange between their mom and dad as they finished up their mac n cheese. Darian jetted up the stairs to change before heading out with what he still hoped was his wife. Lindsay arrived a few minutes later. Lisa gave her some last-minute instructions and she and Darian jumped in the Audi and headed for Herbs.

"You realize those are our children, right. Our impressionable, soak it up like a sponge, children, right," she questioned.

"I know, I know just having a little kid fun," he replied. "Now let's go have some adult fun. How was your day?" he asked. Lisa went on to describe her day from checking emails to laundry to grocery shopping but also commented how great the kids were at helping.

"I'm going to miss them when school starts next week," she said. We just had a great time today. And how did things go at DigiNet today?" she asked.

Darian proceeded to fill her in on the various meetings which took place and the preparation for the Homeland Security job.

"I like your idea of rewarding the company employees financially in the event DigiNet ever hit a windfall," he stated. In a way I want it to be a nice surprise for them someday, but I also don't want to lose any of them and by saying they each will have a little pot of gold at the end of the rainbow is a great way to retain good workers, he said. And we received a nice deposit from the US Government today. The $2,000,000 advance hit our account this morning and Lori has already moved it to an insurance account for safe keeping."

Lisa looked extremely downtrodden.

"What, what is it honey," her husband asked.

"I'm just really concerned. I just don't have a good feeling," she replied.

"About what," he shot back.

"Well," Lisa stammered slowly. "This has been bothering me since we left the house."

"Lisa for Crissakes what the hell is it?" her husband demanded.

"Darian, do you realize we have passed three home decorating stores since we left the house and you have not even noticed?" she said as she finally burst out laughing at her inquisitive husband.

"I'm going to kill you," he said, pretending not to laugh. "I won't bother you; I won't hurt you, but I AM going to kill you," he said shaking his head.

"Too late, we're here," Lisa exclaimed. "Maybe next time," she said with a wink and that captivating little girl smile reserved only for her husband.

Darian pulled the Audi into the parking lot of Herbs and he and Lisa went in through the back door. Seeing Maggie and Joel over near the corner, they waved them over and took seats next to their friends.

"Congratulations buddy on the good news," Joel said as he poured them both a bud light from the half-filled pitcher on the table.

"What good news, asked Darian, glancing across at his wife. After a brief silence, Darian spoke up. "Well indeed, my dad always told me there are three ways to communicate in the world:

Telephone

Television

Tell a Woman!

Lisa pretended to not make eye contact with her husband who just sat there and shook his head again.

"Well thanks, Joel but there's a lot of work to be done," he exclaimed.

"Oh no that's not the good news, Joel replied. "The good news is…. DigiNet is buying!!!" and with that all four of them broke up in laughter. Joel raised his glass and watched as the other three quickly joined in.

"To DigiNet, he said. Congratulations on stepping into the ring,"

"And to Homeland Security," Darian quickly added.

As the evening wore on both couples talked about the neighborhood and how great this summer had been. Although childless, Joel and Maggie loved hearing stories about Josh and Taylor and actually Lisa and Darian considered their two friends to be a sort of an aunt and uncle type to their children. With the flatscreen television within earshot of them, they were able to watch the Indians playing while they ate dinner. The Tribe was batting in the bottom of the seventh and clinging to a 4-3 lead against those pesky division rival Minnesota Twins. Second and third with one out and power hitter Carlos Santana coming to the plate.

Just then the station interrupted the game as there appeared to be some sort of breaking news. The conversation stopped and about half of the restaurant turned its attention to the flatscreen on the wall:

"Let's go live to Kim Ward on the scene now. Kim what do you have,"
came the news anchor's voice.

"Well John, Vermillion police are investigating what appears to be an
accident involving a motor vehicle and possibly an individual out here on a
dirt road right off of Gore Orphanage Road. What is baffling to police is
that what initially looked like a motor vehicle accident is complicated by
the discovery of a .38 caliber handgun. Police say results from ballistics
and fingerprint testing were inconclusive. There appear to be large tire
tracks and some dark green paint chips made right up to this point here,
which very well may have been the point of impact. I'm told the tire tracks
appear to have been made by an oversized vehicle such as a large SUV or
utility truck and police are hopeful they can use the tire tracks and the
paint chips to identify the vehicle that was involved once the tests are
complete. Investigators are still combing the area looking for someone
who may have been injured or clues as to what may have happened.
Vermillion police detective Andrew Judd told me earlier that they are
currently conducting an investigation which includes interviewing all the
local hospitals and businesses, such as this Red Roof Inn behind me, to see
if anyone knows anything further. We'll keep you posted as details become
available. Kim Ward, WKYC news, Vermillion."

Darian's face went blank. Lisa's turned three shades of white. The two looked at each other in a stunned and frightened state of disbelief. Lisa grabbed her purse and headed for the restroom. Darian continued to stare at the flatscreen even after the station returned to the ballgame. After a few minutes, sensing something might be wrong, Maggie excused herself and headed to the restroom as well.

"Boy," Joel said as he watched the story unfold and was oblivious to the recent events in the Reilly's personal lives. "Sounds like some unlucky son-of-a bitch was probably in the wrong place at the wrong time. Gotta wonder if they'll ever find out what happened."

Lisa and Maggie both returned from the ladies room. Lisa's face remained a ghostly pale and she insisted Darian take her home immediately. Both gave Joel and Maggie hugs and headed for their car. As they got into the Audi and pulled out of the parking lot, neither one spoke. Silence seemed to be a recurring theme when handling the messy situation the couple created. The Audi's turn signal clicked repeatedly before they finally turned left out of the parking lot onto Detroit Road. Coming to a traffic light right in front of St. Christopher's Church, Darian reached across the console and held onto his wife's hand. His distressed look matched hers as they blankly stared ahead, each hoping the other would say something.

The subtle sound of another vehicle slowly rolling to a stop caught Darian's attention. As he glanced over Lisa's left shoulder, his heart raced. A Rocky River police car pulled up behind them as the red stop light illuminated their faces through the windshield. Darian and the policeman locked eyes for what seemed like eternity. As he squeezed Lisa's hand a little tighter, he broke the deafening silence that suffocated the car.

"We need to get out of here....."

The light turned green and the Reillys headed for home.

"Now what do we do, cried Lisa as they passed through Rocky River and into Bay Village.

"For now, we keep our eyes open and our mouths shut" replied her husband. "We don't know if this guy is dead or alive," he added.

"I know, I know" she said trying to hold back her frightened tears. That's exactly what I mean. He could be waiting for us on the next block. Darian, we must go to the police. We have to do *something*" she cried.

Darian cautiously made a slow left turn off Windsor Drive and onto Inglewood. As he turned into their driveway, he was careful to do a quick survey of the area anticipating a vengeful Sonny lurking in the darkness. As he pulled into the garage, the couple sat in the car for a minute, trying to figure which direction to turn.

Suddenly the door leading into the house flew open. For a moment, nothing happened. Lisa's heart stopped as she gasped and grabbed her husband's hand firmly. After a moment, Lindsey sheepishly poked her head into the dimly lit garage to show her face to the frightened couple.

"Sorry Mrs. Reilly. I thought I heard the garage door open and I just wanted to make sure it was you," the teenager said quietly. Sensing she had stumbled into a conversation she should not be a part of, she asked if it were ok if she could head home.

"Of course, you can," replied Lisa. "Mr. Reilly will drive you home."

"Oh, that's ok" Lindsey replied. I'm just down at the end of the street and like I always do I can….."

"I'll take you home," commanded Darian in a loud tone. "Hop in. Let's go.

Lisa got out of the car and put her arm around Lindsey almost apologetically.

"It's late. Let Mr. Reilly take you home, honey."

Lindsey nodded and got into the passenger side of the Audi.

Darian, still stressed out by the news report, hardly said anything to Lindsey as he drove her the half mile down the street to her house.

"I'm sorry," he said. "Long day."

"That's ok," replied Lindsey. Thanks for driving me home."

As she got out of the car and headed for the front door, Darian called her back over.

"Here Lindsey," he said. I almost forgot. Thank you again for taking care of the kids" he said as he handed her three $20 bills.

"Thank you, Mr. Reilly," she said as he stepped out of the car. Josh and Taylor were great again as usual. You and Mrs. Reilly sure are lucky."

"You have no idea," Darian said to himself as he turned and headed home.

July 31

The rain seemed to come down harder and harder throughout the night which didn't help the sleepless night Lisa and Darian were experiencing. Not only was Sonny possibly still alive but if that were the case, the whole family could be in grave danger. It was obvious Sonny knew where the Reilly's lived and now Josh and Taylor could be exposed to any sort of unthinkable danger by a ruthless individual.

Darian knew he had to take some immediate and drastic action in order to protect his family. But he was clearly in a dilemma. He couldn't contact the police. He didn't want to disclose this to any of their friends. He was even hesitant to discuss this with his attorney, despite protection under the attorney client privilege.

Since the overnight rain cancelled most of the outdoor activities for the day, the family decided it was best to head out and tackle a few Saturday errands. Josh still had football practice that morning so Lisa dropped him off at the school's practice field a few minutes before 10 am and then promised Darian and Taylor she would meet up with them after her yoga class. This gave her a chance to clear her head and try to help her husband find a clear way out of this mess. Darian texted her that he and Taylor were going to the Barnes and Noble bookstore over at Crocker Park and would meet her and Josh for lunch at TGI Fridays after his practice.

Taylor, as usual, was quick to bury herself in one of several books she had found and seemed quite content to explore them while sitting on one of the couches next to her daddy.

"I'm going over there to the computer honey for a minute. I'll be right over there, ok" Darian said.

"OK Daddy." Taylor replied without even looking up from her book.

Darian wandered over to one of the PC computer stations a few feet away which were partitioned for a bit of extra privacy. Once logged on as a Barnes and Noble guest, he started searching for any sort of information which would lead him to Sonny. If he could get to him first and explain everything, Darian felt he could reason with this guy. Sonny was a businessman, after all.

Nothing came up in trying to locate the henchman. Next, Darian did a google search on various topics from "hitman" to "murder for hire." Most of these sites just had ads for private detectives or security guards for

177

hire or where to purchase handguns for protection. The idea of hiring a private detective had some appeal but then again, Darian didn't want to expose his illegal agreement to anyone and run the risk of either he or Lisa going to jail. If he found someone he could trust, then perhaps the possibility of…..

Taylor!

Darian quickly ran over to the couch and noticed the three books his daughter had been reading appeared to be tossed to one side. Taylor was missing!

"Taylor," Darian called out.

"Taylor." Darian ran up and down the aisles of the children's section, then to the reference desk in the center of the building, and finally to the entrance with the revolving doors.

"Taylor" Darian shouted from just outside the store.

A sense of fear shot through him from head to toe as he frantically ran back inside looking for his six-year-old daughter.

"Sir, what is it, can I help you", said one of the clerks at the checkout desk.

"My little girl was sitting on one of the couches back near the computers reading her book. The books are there but she's gone", he yelled.

Darian and the woman ran toward the back of the store to the couch where Taylor was last seen.

"She was sitting right here. I was at that computer over there and looked up and she was gone", he stammered.

Darian was a mess.

"We'll find her. She has to be here somewhere", the clerk replied.

Reaching for a phone on one of the nearby reference desks, she called to the front desk and immediately ordered a "Code Adam" which sealed the entire store front to back. Soon all customers in the store were alerted and joined in the search for Taylor. The minutes seemed to turn to hours.

"Oh, Taylor where are you my little baby girl," Darian cried out loud as he raced up and down each aisle searching for his little girl in vain.

He needed to call the police. He needed to call Lisa. Thoughts of his little girl being taken by this Sonny character or some other stranger, just gnawed away at him. He could never forgive himself. His sense of panic seemed to grow exponentially by the minute with the idea of never seeing his precious little girl again.

"Can you describe her?" asked the clerk.

"Yes, yes." he said. She's six years old and blonde. She was wearing, let's see…. she was wearing a white, long sleeve sweater. And she had white tennis shoes on," he blurted out.

"She couldn't have gone far," one of the women at the reference desk said.

"Oh my God," the clerk said as she looked behind the panic-stricken father.

Suddenly there was a tug on Darian's sweatshirt.

Taylor!!!

She was standing right behind Darian who quickly scooped her up into his arms and held her tightly as his eyes continued to fill with tears.

"Where were you, sweetie?" asked the disheveled dad. "We were all looking for you." By now a small crowd of people had gathered to witness the emotional father-daughter reunion. Some of the moms were dabbing their eyes with emotion.

"I went to the potty", beamed the six-year-old with a huge smile, as the crowd broke up with laughter and tears of relief. "Mommy always takes me but since you looked busy, I decided to go myself."

Darian slowly let Taylor down but absolutely refused to let go of her hand.

"Remember sweetie, you always need to be with either mommy or me when you go anywhere, ok", Darian warned.

"OK daddy smiled the six-year-old. "I'm hungry. Can we meet mommy and Josh for lunch now?" she asked.

"Of course, we can." said Darian as he let out a huge sigh of relief. "Let's go."

Darian thanked the woman who helped him, along with the other Barnes and Noble people and left with Taylor to meet up with Lisa and Josh.

"Sorry if I scared you Daddy," Taylor said sheepishly as they climbed into Darian's car. Sensing the seriousness of the situation and still thinking about what could have happened, especially with a henchman possibly on the loose, Darian spoke in a direct tone to his six-year-old.

"Sweetie, never, never, ever go off on your own like that. You had me very worried that something bad had happened to you. Promise me you will always stay with either mommy or me when we are out together. There are bad people in the world, and I thought maybe someone had taken you."

"Sorry Daddy," repeated Taylor. "I promise not to do it ever again. I don't want to ever be taken away from you and mommy by a bad guy."

"Me neither," replied the relieved father.

On the three-minute drive over to the restaurant, Darian couldn't help reliving the potential constant reminder that Sonny could have taken his daughter. Staring off into space thinking these horrible thoughts while waiting for the light to change at the intersection of Detroit and Crocker-Bassett Road, a blaring horn from the driver behind him gave him a quick jolt back to reality. Not picking up on Darian's still high level of stress, Taylor asked if she could have one of those tropical drinks with an umbrella when they got to the restaurant.

"Of course, you can, Sweetie," he said. "I can actually use a drink myself right about now."

August 8

The hustle bustle in the Reilly house was characteristic of a typical Sunday afternoon getting ready for Josh's first football game of the season for the Normandy Elementary Rockets. The game was against the reigning city champion St. Margaret Silverhawks and started at 1pm. Darian volunteered to drive Josh early to get him there in plenty of time for pre-game warmups and stretching. Lisa and Taylor would finish cleaning up the huge brunch spread Darian had prepared that morning.

"I'll save your seats," he shouted as he headed out the door to the garage not waiting for a response. But as he went to jump into his Audi, he noticed something strange.

"What is it, Dad," said Josh as he placed his shoulder pads and helmet into the trunk.

"Did you open the garage door this morning, Josh?" Darian inquired.

"No sir," the young lad replied. I took Neely outside this morning but through the back door."

Darian sat in his car, puzzled and a bit concerned.

"Maybe mom opened it when she got up this morning," Josh explained.

Or maybe she had left the garage door open last night before they went to bed, Darian thought to himself. Lisa was prone to leaving lights on, TVs blaring, and doors open at all hours of the day and night while she cleaned the house, cooked or did laundry.

"Probably," Darian said out loud but still wondering. "But anyway, let's get you to the football field in time for pre-game.

Darian always loved sports and now that Josh was becoming somewhat of an athlete himself, he couldn't help but take a little bit of inner pride in his youngster. Josh always got good grades in school and even played the flute with the school orchestra. His participation in sports made him that much more of a well-rounded boy. One who knew right from wrong and good from evil.

The half-smile on Darian's face began to fade as thoughts of Sonny on the loose and possibly bringing harm to either his wife or children.

"You know son," Darian began. "If you ever see something or a situation which looks like something bad might be happening, you know to always come to mom and me, ok."

"What sort of bad do you mean, Dad," inquired the nine-year-old.

Well, Darian replied, there are some bad people in the world. For whatever reason, they will take kids from playgrounds and schoolyards in a second. That's why it's always good to stay in groups and stay with people you know."

"That's what Officer O'Malley said to us when he came to our school on the last day before summer break. He said, 'watch out for stranger danger' or something like that. He said Bay Village was a good area, but bad guys can still come around, so we must be ready. Kind of like playing defense on the football team. You never know what the other side is going to do," said Josh.

Darian had stopped at a traffic light and marveled at the wisdom of his nine-year-old son. Clearly, Josh was aware that even in good areas, bad guys can surface, and bad things can happen to good people.

"You are wise beyond your years buddy" the proud father said smiling.

"Thanks dad," he replied. Now let's go see what St. Margaret's football team will throw at us."

Darian pulled into the parking lot at Bay Village High School and parked close to the where some of the other parents had already assembled.

"Good luck son," Darian said as Josh grabbed his shoulder pads and helmet and ran to join his teammates. Even the short ride to the football field with his son was a roller coaster of emotion ranging from pride to fear to concern.

If this Sonny guy was out there somewhere, no way was he ever going to hurt my family, Darian said to himself.

A frantic and somewhat disheveled mom in a Cleveland Browns ball cap and ponytail and her daughter strolled along the front walkway of the stands scanning the crowd in search of familiar faces. Lisa and Taylor had finally arrived, and just before kickoff. Darian stood and waved his arms in a vain attempt to get his wife's attention. It seemed he was competing with several of Lisa's football mom friends who corralled her into a chit chat session, and he was losing the battle. Knowing his wife better than anyone, he realized she just *had to* exchange a few pleasantries with a few of her close sewing circle friends.

"Hey lady you're blocking my view," he shouted half kidding and several rows up with arms outstretched.

"Look mommy, there's Daddy," Taylor said as she tugged on her mom's sweatshirt.

"Ok, ok, I see him. Let's go Taylor," she said.

The fourth quarter began with both teams locked in a 14-14 tie. Each team had scored two touchdowns yet were able to convert only one of their two-point conversions. Normandy had the ball midway through the fourth quarter and was driving toward the St. Margaret end zone. A second down blitz by the Silverhawks tackled the Rockets' quarterback Alex Reinhold for a huge loss, making a victory seem almost impossible. With the clock running and no timeouts left on a third down play, suspecting another blitz, Normandy head coach John Gallagher called for a quarterback keeper. Sure enough, the Silverhawks sent their safeties on another blitz and Reinhold was running for his life toward the sideline. At the last second, he flipped the ball eight yards downfield and over the head of the charging St. Margaret defensive linemen and into the hands of Normandy tight end, Kevin Allen. Allen scampered fifty-three yards untouched down the field and into the end zone for a Rockets touchdown with just three minutes left in the game. Although the two-point conversion attempt came up short of the goal line, Normandy had a 20-14 lead late in the game.

St. Margaret took the ball at their own twenty-five-yard line and proceeded to march downfield almost at will. The entire Normandy defense, of which Josh was their middle linebacker, was completely exhausted but tried valiantly to hang on. The Silverhawks moved down to the twelve yard line with just thirty-eight seconds to go and seemed like they were about to score. Their running back, JJ King took the ball and ran wide and toward the goal line. Suddenly Josh burst through the block, put a hit on the St. Margaret running back and jarred the ball loose! Josh's buddy and fellow linebacker, Jack Shinkle pounced onto the ball, recovering the fumble for Normandy at the six-yard line, preserving the victory.

The crowd on the Normandy side went wild. The St. Margaret crowd was stunned. Josh and Jack were buried beneath a sea of jubilant teammates as the clock ran out.

Final score: Normandy 20 St. Margaret 14.

"That was quite a lick your boy put on that kid," one of the dads said to Lisa and Darian as they were exiting the stands.

"Well, it's a team game after all," Darian replied, though silently beaming with pride on the inside.

The parents all made their way down from the stands and over to the gathering where the coaches were addressing the players. Although thoroughly exhausted, every boy on the squad was smiling from ear to ear.

As the team finished their post-game prayer on one knee, they all went looking for their parents.

"Great game, buddy," said Darian as he high fived his son.

"You were awesome, sweetie," echoed Lisa.

"Mom," he whispered. "Please don't call me that around the guys, ok," he pleaded.

Taylor grabbed her mom's hand as they headed for the parking lot. Darian carried the water jug while Josh carried his helmet and shoulder pads walking next to his dad. Suddenly Darian stopped dead in his tracks.

"What is it dad," asked Josh.

Darian's face had turned from euphoria to fear. Lisa, noticing her son and husband had stopped a few feet behind, saw the look on Darian's face as he fixated on the figure standing at the deserted north end of the parking lot off in the distance. Her smile had quickly turned to a look of horror as she took note of the individual as well.

Sonny!

The henchman, wearing his signature dark suit and sunglasses, just proceeded to stare them down. Without saying a word, Darian and Lisa each grabbed a child and speed walked to their cars.

"Good to see you Lisa," one of the moms yelled across the way, but Lisa completely ignored her.

Josh put his equipment in his dad's car and jumped in. Lisa and Taylor jumped into the Suburban and quickly locked the doors. Suddenly there was a loud banging on the driver's window. Lisa nearly jumped out of her seat. It was Darian. She rolled down the window nearly out of breath. She and her husband stared at each other looking completely lost and afraid.

"Go straight home. I'm right behind you. Don't go into the house until I pull into the garage, you understand." he commanded.

Lisa nodded silently in agreement. Taylor was safely buckled in the back seat and oblivious to what was going on. Lisa taxied slowly out of the parking lot, glancing again back toward the north end.

He was gone!

Sonny had completely disappeared. He was there sixty seconds ago and now, nowhere to be seen. From the safety of her car, Lisa frantically did a visual search of the entire school complex looking at trees, cars and people still milling around the parking lot but no sign of the henchman anywhere. A sudden horn blast from behind shook her to her core. Darian was directly behind her, motioning her to get moving. Lisa nodded into her rear-view mirror, gave one more quick glance around the outside and pulled out onto Wolf Road and headed home.

"This is crazy," Lisa barked as she and Darian were having a closed bedroom door discussion. "This maniac knows who we are, where we live. Hell Darian, he even knows where Josh plays football on Sunday." What the hell are we going to do?

Darian had so much on his plate with DigiNet and the Government Contract and he sure as heck didn't need some madman terrorizing his family.

"We have to stay calm, he replied. "I'm sure that if I can just make contact with him, I can buy him off, offer him money." His words seemed to fall on deaf ears.

"Darian, I am afraid for my family, for my children. Our children. Christ, we can't even call the police."

"I need to find this idiot, somehow get to him. It always comes down to money," he said.

August 16

A week had passed since Lisa and Darian spotted Sonny at Josh's football game. Things seemed to have calmed down, relatively speaking. Lisa at first refused to leave the house other than taking the kids to school and going to the grocery store. There were crowds of people at both those places with lots of activity, so she figured they were safe places to be. Eventually she worked her way back into her routine. She seemed somewhat resigned to the fact that their lives may never ever get back to normal like they used to be.

Darian as well had not seen nor heard any sign of Sonny since he was spotted at the football game. Given the stress of undertaking an IT government contract and having a madman stalking your family, it paved the way for many a sleepless night. Gerry could tell something was up. He had known Darian for years and the two men rarely kept any secrets from one another.

Darian had called a staff meeting for 9am, customary for a Monday morning at DigiNet. As everyone was filing into the conference room, they couldn't help but notice the commotion in the corner of the room.

"Don't come near me with that thing," Lori pleaded. What the hell are you doing with a gizmo like that," she asked.

"Calm down, calm down. You'll frighten the children," came Gerry's joking response. Besides, it's not activated. My grandfather was a demolition expert during the war, and this was bequeathed to me after he had passed away last year. Pretty cool, eh," he said.

For some reason, Gerry felt the need to bring into the office what was once a live hand grenade from World War. II. Always the gadget guy, he marveled at how he had been able to detonate the other one his grandfather left him by remote control.

"You're sure this puppy isn't live, right?" Darian stammered with caution in his tone.

"Of course not boss," Gerry replied. It was disarmed before it was sent to me. I had a US Army munitions guy detail it to me just to be sure. But being the techno-nerd that you all know that I am, I have developed a remote-control detonator to go with it. In fact, you can *only* set it off with the remote-control detonator and *only* from your phone if you have the app I developed," he boasted. "But on a serious note, this grenade is totally harmless, unless you have the app enabled on your phone... and the password... and you're standing at least 50 feet away but not more than 200 feet from the grenade. It's controlled by radio frequency which requires a minimum of sixteen meters of distance to activate."

"So, I can't hide it in Ben Roethlisberger's helmet and push the button when he's back in the pocket if he's about to beat the Browns?" quipped Darian as marveled at the racquetball sized explosive.

"Oh, I forgot," interjected Gerry. There is no distance limitation when you're blowing up a Pittsburgh Steeler," he said with a straight face.

"Just kidding Vicki," he quickly added with a goofy look to the new software engineer and Pittsburgh native who had just been hired on to help with the government contract.

"I'm sorry Gerry. I didn't hear what you said. I was too busy counting Super Bowl rings," she shot back with a smile.

"Yep, welcome to DigiNet, Vicki," Darian said. Now if show and tell is over people, can we please get down to business?"

The meeting took up most of the morning with Darian leading the strategy session on how to implement their plan to meet the objectives which the Department of Homeland Security had required. After the meeting ended, Darian called Lisa to check in.

"Hey babe, how's it going," he asked as she answered her phone. Everything ok on your end?"

"Yeah, I'm fine," she replied. By the way there seems to be a shake or shimmy when I accelerate my car. I noticed it over the weekend and again this morning on my way home from dropping off the kids. Are we due for a tire rotation or something?

"Actually, I think we just need to get a new set of tires for the Suburban," he said. "We're close to fifty thousand miles on those, so I'll take care of it this week."

"Thanks honey. Actually, Maggie is here, and she and I were just headed out the door for some lunch. Everything going ok there," she asked.

Yes. Very busy with the new government deal and all. I'll fill you in tonight. Love you," Darian said.

"Love you too," came Lisa's reply as she hung up.

Normally, Darian would simply text Lisa to check in and see how her day was going but in lieu of this recent sighting of Sonny the madman he felt better calling her and was relieved that she and Maggie had plans for lunch. Darian still had one eye on DigiNet and one eye on Sonny. He knew this person wasn't going to go away anytime soon and he needed to fix this problem now.

August 18

The pickup line at Normandy seemed to take a little longer than usual. Due to the constant downpour which had started about noon, there were more parents picking up their kids who would normally be letting them walk home if the weather co-operated. A Bay Village police car was parked a block before the entrance of the school, with flashers going. A clap of thunder signaled that the rainstorm was not going to let up anytime soon. Lisa was concerned that Josh and Taylor would be wet mops by the time they would reach her car. And to complicate matters, there was a slight fender bender right at the main entrance off Normandy Road causing bumper to bumper traffic all the way back to Dover Center Road.

Bad weather, car accidents and slick conditions. Let me just get my kids and get out of here, Lisa said to herself.

Normally Josh and Taylor are able to walk down the main driveway entrance from the school and jump into their mom's car. But the driving rain made this impossible. Lisa had her wipers going and kept her eyes on the main entrance to the school which had a large canopy over it for times like these, thank goodness. As she slowly navigated the large six-hundred-foot semi-circle driveway and then came to another brief stop, she glanced across the street and saw something which sent shivers down her spine.

Sonny!

There he stood, a hundred yards away in that same dark coat, in the driving rain, and was staring right at her!

Lisa was panic stricken. And helpless. She started to freak out without her kids safely in the car and this madman was standing across the street from their school! How could he know where her kids go to school? She was terrified. Just then a blast of a horn from behind reminded her to keep moving as she had become paralyzed and failed to keep her car moving along this slow caravan.

Suddenly Josh and Taylor emerged from the school's main entrance with Josh holding his sister's hand and pointing out his mom's car to Mrs. Susan, one of his teachers.

"Quick kids get in. Quickly, quickly," she commanded. Thinking their mom was trying to move them along rapidly due to the storm, Josh and Taylor thought nothing of it, jumped into the Suburban and closed the door. Lisa carefully maneuvered her way down the other side of the semicircle driveway and looked to her left across the street through the pouring rain.

He was gone!

Nothing. How could he have disappeared that quickly? Waiting at the traffic light to turn onto Normandy Road, she visually scoured the entire scene.

Nothing. Still experiencing an extremely high sense of panic, she accidentally made a right turn on red and headed home.

"Kids put all your wet things in the laundry room, and I'll get to them in a minute," Lisa said as they entered their house. "Get started on your homework and I'll be right there. I need to call Daddy first," she barked out.

"I saw him! I saw him," Lisa cried into the phone to her husband. "He was at the kids' school. I was waiting in line in my car to pick the kids up and I saw him. He was waiting across the street right on Normandy staring me down. Darian, he knows where our kids go to school!" she yelled almost hysterically seated in Darian's den.

"Stay there. Make sure all the doors are locked," he commanded. I'm on my way home now."

Ten minutes later, Darian pulled into the garage, closing it behind him.

"Daddy," Taylor shouted as she jumped into Darian's waiting arms. "Why are you home so early," she asked.

"Yeah dad," Josh added. Normally you don't show up until dinnertime.

"Well," said Darian, "We, uh...had a um...a power outage at the office so I sent everyone home. Besides, on a yucky night like this there's no place I rather be than with you guys and mom," he added. By the way, where is mom," he asked.

"She's upstairs talking to Grammy and Pappy," Josh responded.

"Thanks buddy. Keep working on your homework while I go upstairs and talk to mom," he said.

"I didn't say anything about this to mom and dad," Lisa explained as Darian entered the room. "I just called them to see if they were open to taking Josh and Taylor for a long weekend. Oh Darian, I am so scared," she said as she buried her head in his chest and held on crying uncontrollably. "He knows where our kids are. Who knows what this man is capable of? We've got to protect them," she pleaded with him as she continued to sob.

"I know, I know," he acknowledged. "Tomorrow's Thursday and they have Friday off, don't they? They can miss one day of school," he reasoned.

"Please don't let them hurt my babies," she cried. "Don't let him come near my babies. Please Darian. PLEASE," she screamed. "Don't let them hurt my babies!"

Lisa was hysterical. Darian got her to lie down on the bed and covered her with a soft blanket. She just kept rocking back and forth uncontrollably.

"Please don't let them hurt my babies," she continued to wail to herself.

Darian sat beside her and quietly stroked her long dishwater blonde hair until she seemed to drift off to sleep. The love of his life, the mother of his children had been driven to hysterics and it seemed he was powerless to do anything about it. He was equally a mess about the situation but had to hold it together for the sake of his wife and children. Quietly he left a small night light on for her and closed the door as he headed down to see the kids.

"Mommy's not feeling well, guys," he said to his children. "Let's try to keep it down so she can sleep for a while. Since it's such a gloomy night, why don't we order pizza, ok?" he asked.

"Yeah pizza," said Josh. "From Frankie's dad?" he asked.

"Of course. The best pizza in town. And I'll have them deliver it so we can stay inside tonight, how's that?" Darian said with a half-smile.

"Great," said Taylor. I love Frankie's,"

Darian ordered the pizza along with a chopped salad for Lisa and quietly snuck upstairs to check on her. She was sound asleep which was probably what she needed the most right about now. Trying to collect himself from the afternoon's events, he texted Gerry saying he had to take care of a family emergency and won't be back in the office til tomorrow.

"NP Hope all is ok," came the reply.

Twenty minutes later the doorbell rang.

"Can I get it, can I get it" screamed Taylor as she raced toward the front door.

"Taylor," Darian commanded. "Do not go *near* the front door. I will answer the door."

Taylor shyly turned away, a little hurt from her dad's harsh tone of voice. Darian turned and knelt down and tried to comfort the six-year-old.

"Sweetie, you know we never answer the door until we know who it is, remember," he said softly. Taylor nodded in agreement.

"Come in, come in, please," said Darian to the pizza delivery boy.

"It's prepaid sir so you don't owe anything."

Darian reached into his wallet and gave the driver a $10 bill. "It's such a crummy night. Take this and be safe out there, buddy," Darian said as he handed the young man the tip.

"Thank you, sir," came his reply. I guess you're right. You can never be too safe these days. Have a great rest of your evening".

"No, you sure can't," Darian said to himself as he closed the front door and locked it securely. You sure as hell can't these days."

Josh and Taylor finished their pizza while Darian went back and forth between focusing on his children and staring out the kitchen window at the rain still coming down.

"Guys, mom and I have a little surprise for you." How would you both like to spend this weekend at Grammy and Pappy's?"

Both Josh and Taylor jumped with enthusiasm. The thought of spending a whole weekend with their grandparents brought immediate smiles to the youngsters' faces.

"And since you have no school on Friday, mom and I thought it would be a special treat to have you both miss a day of school and leave tomorrow."

The two children could not contain themselves. "Wow this is great," Josh exclaimed.

"When can we go daddy? Taylor asked.

"Mommy will drive you up to Grammy and Pappy's tomorrow so you can have a nice long weekend up there with them, ok" he replied. "But first, Darian commanded, "we need to get all our schoolwork done before we leave. We need to go over your math homework Taylor," he said. "Why don't you bring it down here and I'll help you with it, ok."

"Ok daddy," the six-year-old replied as she scampered off.

"Josh, do you have any homework to do," he asked his son.

"Just some reading in science, Dad," he replied. We're learning about gasses and explosions and stuff. Pretty cool,"

"I loved science when I was your age," Darian replied. To me it was never boring.

Josh cleared his place at the table and started to head to the family room to concentrate on his reading.

"Please be very quiet buddy. Mom isn't feeling well, and I think she needs her rest."

"Ok dad," his son replied.

"It's ok, kids," came Lisa's voice as she walked into the kitchen.

"Mommy, mommy," cried Taylor as she rushed over to give her a hug. "Are you ok? Daddy said you were sick."

"I'm fine guys," Lisa said as she exchanged a cautionary glance with her husband. "I had a little headache but I'm feeling better now."

"Is it true mom," Josh inquired as he heard his mother come into the kitchen. Are we really going to spend the weekend at Grammy and Pappy's?"

"I think that's a great idea," Lisa said as she caught on to the situation. You both will have a wonderful time and Dad and I will come get you on Sunday."

Both kids finished their homework and headed to their rooms to help their mom pack their suitcases. After the kids were tucked in for the night, Lisa joined her husband in the kitchen to discuss their plan to protect their children.

"Are you sure we're doing the right thing," she asked.

"We have no choice," Darian shot back. "We need to do whatever it takes to protect our children."

"But what can we do?" Lisa replied with tears in her eyes. They can't stay at mom and dad's forever? How can we stop this madman?"

"Whatever it takes," Darian said as he stared off through the kitchen window and into the night.

"Whatever it takes."

August 19

"Bye daddy, I love you and I'll miss you," Taylor said as she climbed into the Suburban.

"I miss you already, sweetie," came Darian's reply as he gave her one last hug. Josh had just thrown his suitcase into the back of the car and came around to say goodbye to his dad.

"I'll miss you, big guy," Darian said as he gave his son a hug. "You look after your sister, ok," he asked. "And try to save me some fudge from the chocolate factory, ok," he said with a smile.

"Right dad. Of course. No problem. You can count on me," Josh said with a kid's wink and a smile.

Lisa gave Darian a hug and kiss before climbing into her car. It was shortly before 10 am.

"Everything's going to be alright," he said to his wife as she sighed heavily. "I'm headed to the office now, but I'll be home early, ok?" he said.

"I know, I know. After I drop off the kids, I'm going over to Nick's to have the tires replaced so I probably won't be home until the afternoon. See you tonight. Love you." she said.

"Love you too honey," Darian said as he gave her another kiss.

"Bye Neely. Take good care of Daddy while we're gone," Taylor shouted from the SUV as it was backing out of the driveway.

As soon as Lisa and the kids waved goodbye and were out of sight, Darian did a quick search of the house and grounds for any signs of an intruder. He knew Sonny was a criminal, but he was also a businessman and for the right price, he could be bought off. At least Darian had convinced himself that this was the case.

Arriving at the DigiNet offices a little later than usual, he saw the staff was already in full swing. The Department of Homeland Security required his undivided attention as the details of such a job seemed to be growing exponentially. Gerry stuck his head into his boss' office minutes after arriving just to make sure all was ok.

"Had a minor family emergency I had to take care of," Darian explained. "Nothing I couldn't handle. Now let's find out the sources of these potential IT breaches in our government's security system," he said to his confidant.

The two men spent the remainder of the morning going over potential and existing breaches of IT security as it pertained to their new favorite customer. Lori would occasionally join them to help direct the rest of the staff on their assigned duties. This was a huge undertaking and everyone at DigiNet was consumed by their tasks at hand. Vicki drew upon her experience at the Department of Veteran Affairs in Pittsburgh to relate how similar types of cyber security breaches can be avoided in the future. Educated as a computer software engineer at the University of Pittsburgh, she graduated fourth in her class out of eighty-four, mostly male students. Between her rigorous education at Pitt, coupled with her VA experience, she was an invaluable asset for Darian and the rest of DigiNet. The company was certainly glad to have her.

Lisa jumped onto the eastbound ramp of Interstate 90 near Detroit Road, merged into the mid-morning traffic, fairly light at this hour and settled into the forty-five-minute drive east to Conneaut. She had already called the school and told them both Josh and Taylor were going to be absent and tried to keep her mind focused on a few of the other details she had to accomplish today. Keeping an eye out for any suspicious looking drivers on the highway or any vehicles which may appear to be following her, she reasoned the further she and the children got from Bay Village, the safer they would be.

A few minutes later she passed the merging of I-90 and I-71, then downtown Cleveland, past Cleveland State University then around Deadman's curve and finally eastbound onto the Lakeland Freeway. The beautiful view of Lake Erie to her left, along with both Josh and Taylor immersed in their books, seemed to provide her with a much-needed sense of calm.

Everything's going to be alright she said to herself, echoing Darian's words. She knew somehow, someway this would work itself out. After all, Darian had now come into a lot of money and this Sonny character was a businessman. Certainly, there was a dollar figure that would simply make this guy just go away. But the inability to locate him and the uncertainty of the situation along with the potential danger to her family kept her on edge. She had to make sure everything appeared normal when they arrived at her parents' house.

"How much further mom," asked Josh as his book was beginning to bore him.

"There it is. There's our exit one mile ahead," Lisa said with a feigned smile. Turning off the freeway and onto Ohio Route 7 north to Conneaut, she heard a slight rumble from one of the rear tires. As Route 7 turned into Main St as they approached the Conneaut city limits, she slowed down to 25 miles per hour and the peculiar noise seemed to go away. Left on Clark Street and then right on Benjamin Street, Lisa pulled into her parents' driveway just before 11 am.

"Look it's Booker Brown," Josh exclaimed as he saw the tail wagging golden retriever run up to the car to greet them. Both Josh and Taylor were smothered with kisses from the playful dog, still only seven months old but quite the welcomed addition to Lisa's parents' household.

"Grammy," shouted Taylor as she escaped from the dog and ran into her grandmother's waiting arms.

"Hello sweetheart," Lisa's mom replied. How's my girl?" Josh tore himself away from Booker Brown to run and give his grandmother a hug.

"You both promised me you wouldn't grow up *this* fast, and now look at you! she exclaimed.

"Hi mom," Lisa said as she gave her mother a kiss and a hug. "Where's dad?"

"He's out back by the pool talking to the maintenance man,"

"Hey, there's my kiddy bums," came the rough and tough voice of Lisa's father as he came around the corner of the house.

"Pappy," cried Taylor as she and Josh both jumped into the man's arms.

"Hey dad," Lisa shouted to her attentive-to-the-grandchildren father. "You're about to have your hands full for the next few days," she added.

"That's ok by me," Lisa's dad replied as he gave her a hug. "How are you honey," he asked with a big smile.

"We're fine. Everything's fine. We're ok," Lisa replied with a bit of a stammer.

"Now look pumpkin," Lisa's father said to her after a long pause with a stern look as he put his arm around her. I know when something's eating you. Are you worried about how to spend all that DigiNet money," he asked with a laugh?

"Steve!" yelled Lisa's mother.

"There is something, Dad. I hope there's a way to get this fixed but I'm not sure." Lisa replied. "I heard a bit of a rumble from the rear of the car as I got off the highway and I wanted to be sure the tires were ok to get me back home."

"Let me take a look," came his serious reply.

Lisa and her dad walked back to the Suburban parked in the driveway while Josh and Taylor grabbed their suitcases out of the back of the car.

"Actually, I'm headed back home to the tire place near our house as soon as I leave here to get a complete set of new tires, but I wanted to make sure they were ok to get me there," she stated.

"Hmmm," here dad paused after examining the four tires. Your front tires are ok fine, a little bald but ok but this right rear looks a little worn," he said. "That was the rumble you heard. You should have plenty of tread all the way around to get you home. But why don't we take the car over to one of the local tire places and get them replaced while you're here. You can stay and have lunch and then pick up the car later," he said.

"Actually, I made the appointment near our house to get the tires replaced and then I have a million things to do," Lisa said. Bedsides, I'm sure you have big plans for the weekend with these two," as she pointed to her two children eyeballing the swimming pool.

"Well at least let me follow you back home so I know you made it safely," her dad replied.

"Dad, that's an hour each way with traffic. I can't ask you to do that. I'll be fine. Really," Lisa pleaded.

"Promise me if you have a problem on the way home, you'll call me, ok honey," he asked.

"I promise, Dad.," Lisa replied.

A few minutes later, Lisa gave Josh and Taylor both a big hug and kiss goodbye and headed back home. Catching a little of the noon traffic as she passed through downtown Cleveland, she headed west on I-90 through Lakewood to the Rocky River exit. She thought about stopping into DigiNet and maybe asking Darian to give her a lift home from the tire place but then thought better of it. This Homeland Security Contract was a huge deal for the company and her husband didn't need to be disturbed.

Lisa arrived at Nick's Tire and Auto Repair in Rocky River shortly before 12:30 pm. Nick and Gina Bovenzi were friends of the Reillys, and Nick always had taken care of their cars for years.

"Hey Nick," Lisa said as she strolled into the owner's office.

"Hey yourself, lady," the middle-aged owner replied. "How about a hug," he said playfully as he was covered with grease and oil from a recently completed ring and valve job.

"How about a rain check til Saturday night when you and your wife show up for beer and Euchre," she quipped.

"You gotta deal," Nick replied. "Anything I need to know about the car other than replacing the tires," he asked.

"I don't think so but if you think it needs something else just take care of it," Lisa said.

Years ago, when the Reillys had just moved to Northern Ohio, they had an old Toyota in which the brakes started squealing. Being new to the area, they found a Tire and Auto Replacement Center nearby where they lived at the time and took it in for service. The manager came out a few minutes later and said they needed their brakes redone front and back at a cost of over $600. Sensing a need for a second opinion, Darian looked in the phone book at the time and found a small auto repair shop in Rocky River. He took it over to have the car's brakes assessed and a few minutes later a dark tanned, Italian looking man came out to speak to him.

"I'm Nick, I'm the owner," he said.

"Nick nice to meet you. I'm Darian. How bad are the brakes?" Darian asked with a wince.

"Your brakes are fine. Just a little brake dust. Fifteen bucks," the man said.

Darian could not believe his ears. "Are you sure," he gasped. The other place said I needed brakes replaced front and back."

"Come over here. Let me show you something," Nick said as he motioned Darian over to where his car was being serviced. "See here. Plenty of pad for at least another 8,000 miles," the mechanic said. When he showed him how much pad he had left on his brakes, Darian at that point knew he had a friend for life and would never take any of their cars anywhere else for service.

Nick built his business up over the years by his honesty and integrity. Later he and his wife Gina became close friends of the Reillys and even introduced them to other local business friends around the community. Darian, always the competitor, has still yet to beat Nick at Euchre!

"You need a ride home, girl," Nick shouted to Lisa over the sound of the unusually loud air guns.

"I'm good. I've got a rideshare waiting. No worries. We'll see you Saturday," she shouted back.

"Saturday it is," Nick said as he disappeared into one of the pits requiring his attention.

Standing outside waiting for her ride, Lisa sent a text to her dad saying she made it safely to the tire repair place and that she was fine. She then saw an email from Normandy Elementary School's Friday Folder giving assignments for Josh and Taylor for the week ahead as she half noticed the grey sedan pull up along the front door where she was waiting. She jumped into the back of the waiting car which sped off immediately.

"Good afternoon sir," Lisa said to the driver without looking up.

"Afternoon ma'am," replied the driver, focusing on the road.

After she finished reading the school email, she looked up and noticed they were getting onto the freeway but headed away from Bay Village.

"Excuse me," Lisa said as the driver merged with the highway traffic. "I think you're going the wrong way. You were supposed to go west on I-90, not east. I think you went the wrong way."

"I don't think so ma'am," the driver responded as he snatched her phone right out of her hand.

The driver then removed his sunglasses.

It was Sonny...

"These devices they have in the ioT sector are lacking encryption which is why their whole system could be compromised," Gerry barked out to everyone at the meeting.

"You've got to remember, hoss. This is a government operation. If it weren't, we probably wouldn't be sitting here trying to figure out this mess," Darian reminded him.

The meeting between the two, along with a host of other support staff members had dragged on since lunch time. Everyone was getting a little spent yet still felt the need to voice his or her opinion on how to remedy the US Department of Homeland Security's cyber security breaches.

It was 4:10 pm. Not knowing how much longer this meeting was going to last, Darian ordered everyone to take a ten-minute break. He sent a quick text to Lisa letting her know he may be running a little late but should be home closer to six or seven at the latest. Checking on a few emails he managed to send out a response to the City of Lakewood letting them know that DigiNet would be starting next week to fix their court's security system. As he headed back into the meeting he glanced at his phone and noticed he hadn't heard from Lisa who was always quick to respond to his text messages, especially near the end of the day.

Reminding himself that she was without kids for an afternoon, he smiled thinking she must be out shopping with Maggie and probably got sucked into a happy hour somewhere over at Crocker Park. Gerry motioned him back into the meeting as Darian, keeping with tradition, was again the last one to rejoin the group.

"They are using a UDP which makes them particularly vulnerable to source address spoofing making it easier for attackers to send data packets that appear to originate from a different IP address," Gerry said as the meeting commenced. "When the attacks are against UDP-based servers such as DNS, multicast DNS, the Network Time Protocol, the

Simple Server Discovery Protocol, or the Simple Network Management Protocol, the effects can be increased and amplified."

"And the worst news is, our US Government is oblivious to this," Darian interrupted. "Can our network breach protocol interrupt their routing traffic? Wouldn't that be the most efficient way to solve this?" he asked his friend.

By 5:30 the two men along with Lori, Vicki and the other staff members had had enough. Their tongues were tired, and all were exhausted. Darian broke up the meeting, thanked everyone for a job well done and told them all to head home and have a safe evening. Back in his office he replied to a few more emails and checked on a few government websites just as Gerry stuck his head in the door.

"Those damn hackers," Gerry said half-jokingly. "They certainly do make it interesting for us geeks, do they not?" he asked his boss rhetorically.

"They certainly do," Darian replied as he kept scrolling through his phone without looking up. Although, if it weren't for the bad guys, we good guys would be on the unemployment line" he said as he stood up to leave.

"Maybe we could just send them Grandpa's hand grenade then hit the send button and kaboom!" Gerry added with his arms flailing dramatically.

"Did you really design an app to trigger that thing," Darian inquired.

"Once the app is enabled, you don't do a thing. You just hit your send button and that old barn way in the back of my property is history. If you want, come on over this weekend and I'll show you. I was planning to tear it down anyway and the fire department just gave me permission to blow it up," Gerry continued.

"Perhaps another weekend," said Darian as he cautiously looked closer at the app on Gerry's phone. "I have a certain phobia to fire and explosions. If this thing is going to blow up your barn, I want to be at least a football field away," he explained. "And besides, the kids are at Lisa's parents for the weekend so yours truly has to scoot," he said with a bit of a twinkle in his eye.

"No kids for the weekend, eh," Gerry echoed. Better be on your way boss. No telling what kind of excitement she has in store for you tonight," he said with a laugh.

"Funny thing is, she got the tires replaced on her car and then I think she was having lunch with Maggie. Her location service says she is still in Rocky River over by Nick's. Oh, wait she's probably picking up the car. No worries. Have a good one my friend. We'll tackle the bad guys in the morning."

Gerry jumped into his truck and zoomed out of the parking lot for home. Darian locked the office, jumped into his Audi and headed for home. A moment later Lisa was calling.

"Where have you been babe? I hadn't heard from you all day. Thought maybe you had forgotten all about me," Darian said as he spoke into the phone.

"Oh, I didn't forget about you," came the frighteningly familiar voice from the past on the other end. "Like I said, you rich guys think you got all the power. Well, I've got the power now. And your girl," he said.

Darian froze. He had to pull off the side of the road to collect himself.

"What's going on?" Darian replied. "Where's my wife?"

"Here's the deal," Sonny continued.

"Let me talk to Lisa," Darian shouted into the phone.

"Sure. No problem. She's on speaker now. Say hi darlin', he said with a sickening laugh.

"Darian help me please," Lisa mumbled. "He's serious. He says he'll kill me then you then the kids. He's going to…."

"That's right Darian sweetheart," Sonny said cynically as he snatched the phone from her.

"Wait. Please. Wait. I have money now. I can pay you. Don't hurt her. I'm begging you please don't hurt my wife," Darian bellowed into the phone.

"Here's the deal, chief. Me and the wife here are going to relive us some old times. After all, I think I owe her one after she nailed me with the car a few weeks ago. But I'll tell you what. Just to show you what a nice guy I am, I'll make you a deal. There's an old farmhouse right near the spot where your pretty Mrs. here nearly took me out. Meet me there in an hour and she's all yours. Oh, and by the way, bring an extra $50,000 in cash. Got it?" he growled.

"Wait, wait, I need more time than that to….:

"ONE HOUR," Sonny barked angrily into the phone. "Not a minute later." And he hung up.

Glancing at his watch Darian saw that it was 7:12 pm.

He *really* had to think clearly and move fast now.

By now it was near 8 pm and dusk was starting to set in, normal for this time of year in Northeastern Ohio. The beautiful sunset over the western edge of Lake Erie was overshadowed by the impending danger which lay ahead. Darian pulled onto the ramp off Route 2, the same exit he took weeks ago when left for the hotel and was on the run from Sonny. Now he had to make the biggest deal of his life. Random thoughts kept racing through his mind. Should I call the police? Was Lisa ok? Was she still alive? Is this a trap? Can I really trust this thug who I don't even know?

Turning left onto Vermillion Rd and passing that same Red Roof Inn, he turned right onto Gore Orphanage Road close to the deserted spot where he and Lisa had met Sonny before. Pulling into a field next to the old collapsing abandoned farmhouse, Darian parked his car, got out with backpack in hand and waited. Glancing at his phone, the time said 8:04 pm. Only the faint sound of trucks on the highway a few miles off in the distance could be heard. Things were eerily quiet. Not a good sign. He looked around but did not move, for he thought for sure he was being watched. No hills or valleys. No trees or bushes. Just wide-open space. No places for the local police or sheriff to hide. A perfect place to make a simple exchange. Or worse.

"Darian," came Lisa's faint, distant cry. "Darian," she repeated almost as if on cue.

"Lisa", Darian shouted. "Lisa, are you alright?"

"She's fine chief, came Sonny's ugly raspy voice. "Just keep walking. That's right. Baby steps."

Lisa, with the henchman holding her at gunpoint, finally emerged from the rear of the old farmhouse walking carefully toward Darian.

"I have the money. Let's do this and get it over with," Darian shouted, walking gingerly toward the henchman. "It's all here. It's all yours. I'm not armed. Just let my wife go."

"Let's see the money," Sonny shouted back as they were now only a few yards apart. "Drop the bag right where you are," he commanded.

Darian carefully lowered the sack to the ground, leaving it on the grassy field.

"Now move away," Sonny said as he held the gun to Lisa's left temple.

Darian retreated slowly from the spot where he had left the backpack. Sonny forced Lisa to the ground, ordering her to pick it up and lay it by his feet.

"Open it," the henchman yelled.

As she began to unzip the main compartment a covering of several $50 dollar bills could be seen near the opening.

Suddenly, Lisa was released by the henchman. Running over to Darian now only a few yards away, she jumped into his arms and looked back at Sonny.

"It's ok, it's ok, honey. It's going to be alright, Darian reassured her. "Are you ok? Did he hurt you?" he asked her.

"I'm ok, I guess," the frightened woman replied. "Now can we just get out of here?" she begged.

"Let's go," her husband replied as he cradled her protectively while turning toward the car.

"Not so fast, chief," came Sonny's raspy voice. "You don't actually think I can leave any witnesses behind do ya?" he laughed. "Besides, I believe I owe you and the Mrs. one from our last outing out here together. Thanks to you lady, I'm now walking with a limp for the rest of my life. Both of you now, down on your knees," he commanded.

"You can't do this. You can't do this. Please," Darian pleaded. "We had a deal. You've got your money. Please just let us go. Even if we wanted to go to the police, we're just as guilty as you are," Darian yelled.

"Ya see," Sonny responded. It's like I said. You rich guys think you have all the power. Now who has the power now?" he shouted while pointing his gun at the defenseless couple.

"Please, please, let us just say goodbye to our kids, please," Darian cried out like a condemned man. "We just want to tell them that we love them," he said.

"Forget it. I don't have time for any bleeding-heart message," he said. Like I told you once before:

"Nobody ever breaks the contract....... Nobody," the henchman yelled as he slowly took aim.

Lisa buried her head next to Darian's shoulder, shaking as she closed her eyes. Sonny stood there, backpack in one hand and his gun pointed right at them with the other.

"I love you, Darian," Lisa cried.

"I love you Lisa," Darian replied.

And then.......

BOOM!!!

The sudden noise sounded like a huge clap of thunder and rattled a flock of geese who were gathered nearby, causing them to take to the skies. Lisa looked up after hearing the thunder-like crash, her tear-stained cheeks and swollen red eyes looking on in amazement. Suddenly, from behind they saw someone getting out of Darian's car.

Gerry!

"I'll be dipped in shit," Gerry said as he walked over to the couple. "This sucker actually works," he said glancing at the app on his phone. "I sure as hell am glad that son of a bitch didn't wander too much further away. A few more steps and he'd been out of range to enjoy Grandpa's hand grenade."

"You're glad???" Darian exclaimed.

The three of them slowly wandered over to the now lifeless body of Sonny the henchman who had been blown right out of his shoes. Scattered among the area were bits and pieces of Darian's old backpack, along with the latest edition of *The Plain Dealer* which had been stuffed inside.

"Let's go," Darian commanded.

The three individuals jumped into the Audi and sped away. Turning left onto Gore Orphanage Road, they all looked back to see just a small billow of smoke coming from the deadly site way off in the distance.

"This would make a helluva James Bond story," Gerry said from the backseat as they merged onto the freeway. "Who was that dude, anyway?" he asked.

"You have no idea, and you have no idea," Darian replied, as he and Lisa glanced at each other.

He hit the gas as the three of them headed for home.

The End

.

Made in United States
Orlando, FL
18 April 2022

16949020R00124